IRRESISTIBLY ALONE

JULIE COOPER

Quills & Quartos
PUBLISHING

Edited by Lucy Marin, Jan Ashton, and Regina McCaughey-Silvia

Cover by Josephine Blake, Covers & Cupcakes

ISBN 978-1-956613-64-3 (ebook) and 978-1-956613-65-0 (paperback)

To Dennis,
For better or for worse, for richer or for poorer, in sickness and in health, for time and for all eternity.

TABLE OF CONTENTS

One

November 26, 1811

When Elizabeth was summoned to her father's book-room, she easily—and immediately—went, although she was feverishly adding embroidery to her bodice for tonight's ball.

Papa often had her fetched when he read something particularly ironic in one of his newspapers, and they both enjoyed a good laugh; while she might share more in his amusement tomorrow than during so hectic a time, she was a dutiful daughter and cherished the marks of her father's favour.

"Close the door, Lizzy," Mr Bennet said—rather brusquely, she thought. Elizabeth took her usual chair across from the walnut desk, carved—she had been told many times—from one of Longbourn's trees which had been struck by lightning and toppled onto the house, nearly destroying it a hundred years past. And yet, here they were, still, Bennets of Longbourn.

"We are resilient, at least," her father always said.

She glanced up at his profile and saw that he was in

1

one of his impatient moods. They usually proceeded from being forced to perform a duty he found unappealing—which was, in truth, most of them. He much preferred reading about farming methods and scientific means of increasing yields than troubling himself to institute them. However, the black armband he still wore reminded her of the funeral service he had attended last month; his sorrow could not have helped his state of mind.

Strictly speaking, he need not have donned any black at all, much less wear it for so long a period; the Gouldings were distant cousins on his maternal line, once or twice removed. But he and old Mr Goulding had been friends since boyhood, although the latter was his elder by eight or nine years. The accidental death of Mr Goulding's only son, Reginald, was tragic, and she knew Papa mourned with his friend.

"I shall come right to the point," her father said, his voice stern. "You are to be married."

"What?" To Elizabeth, the words sounded as if from a foreign tongue, in no language she could recognise. "What was that?"

"You heard me. I have arranged a match for you."

At her obvious continued confusion, however, he dropped some of his severity. "You are nearly one-and-twenty. I cannot provide for you in the case of my death and would not have you cast upon the world."

"My uncle Gardiner—"

"Has four children of his own to provide for. He is prospering, yes, and by the time he is my age, I expect his position to be a good one. But it would be wrong to expect him to care for you, your sisters, and your mother. He would do it, but it would be an enormous burden, and his own family would suffer."

A terrible feeling crept up her spine, and her voice came out as a whisper. "Mr Collins is ridiculous, Papa. I could never like or respect him!"

"Credit me with more understanding than to yoke you to a fool, if you please."

Elizabeth could only gape at him. If not Mr Collins, then who? And why, if he had intended to arrange her a marriage, had he never mentioned the fact? She ought to have been preparing her mind to accept the possibility for years!

Confusion gripped her, the number of unknowns almost too alarming to consider.

"Perhaps you did not know that Haye-Park is entailed."

A sickening possibility crept into her mind, but she shook her head against it. *No, no, no.*

"I *told* Goulding he and Reginald ought to break it, but he failed to heed my advice. Had a son too early in his marriage to feel the pinch, I suppose. Reginald was equally blind. A young man in his position ought not to have stupidly put off marriage until his thirtieth year."

"Perhaps Mrs Goulding—"

"They were holding out hope, but as of this morning, it is gone. Mrs Goulding is not with child. There is no heir."

Elizabeth bit her lip. Mr Goulding had been a

widower this last decade; as far as she could tell, he had never considered remarriage. She knew he was well past fifty, but he could easily pass for a man ten years older. A tall, if somewhat stooped man, his grey, bushy eyebrows rimmed deep-set, tiny eyes, and spectacles were always perched on his rather bulbous nose. Constantly afflicted with the gout, his favourite dinner table conversation was speaking—at length—about the various remedies with which he attempted to cure it.

He was no one's ideal bridegroom, even had she been twenty years older. Her father surely could not mean for her to marry him!

"Papa, you are not suggesting I—"

"Yes, Elizabeth. Goulding and I have agreed that you will wed."

"You cannot be serious! Without warning or discussion? Without even *asking* me? Perhaps you have not considered what would happen if I produce no male child—or Mr Goulding cannot retain the wherewithal to *make* one? I would be worse off than ever," she cried. "With an inheritance that does not truly belong to him and all the best years of my life devoted to an elderly man who cannot supply me with the required offspring, upon his death, I will find myself homeless and as helpless as I ever was, with no option but to beg his unknown relations for shelter and sustenance."

"Nonsense! Haye-Park is a prosperous estate," he argued. "I would, of course, ensure that your jointure is generous and a dower house provided. You will be able to assist your sisters, even, I do not doubt. Besides, he is not so elderly as all that."

She only stared at him; surely he understood that she looked upon Mr Goulding as an uncle, or even a fatherly figure. The very thought of becoming his wife caused a nearly uncontrollable bout of nausea.

"I will not do it," she managed. "It is impossible." The future, which a few minutes ago had looked pleasant and ordinary, if unexciting, suddenly appeared as a black, gaping hole. *Nothing* would convince her to agree to the match; her father might try to convince her it was for the best, but she never would accept it.

Mr Bennet's face hardened. "There is, unfortunately, no choice in the matter. I owe him a debt I cannot repay. He has called in his markers. If you do not marry him, I am ruined, and all our family with me."

"What?" Elizabeth closed her eyes, feeling the trap closing in around her.

"I shall not repeat myself. You *will* marry Mr Goulding. He is rich, and you may have more fine clothes and carriages than even Jane, should she marry Mr Bingley. You will become mistress of a house larger than Netherfield and possess anything money can buy. Any refusal proves you ungrateful and childish, behaving as though I am throwing you out into the hedgerows."

At this unfeeling charge, she reared back. "Since when do fine clothes and carriages equal happiness? Is there not some other way to repay your debt to him? Mary, Kitty, or even Lydia might cherish the opportunity to become mistress of Haye-Park. Why not at least *ask* a daughter who might *be* grateful?"

He looked away. "Your sisters are too young, he says. He will only accept marriage to you or Jane. Those were his conditions, not mine. I have no choice. *You* have no choice."

"Because Jane is already betrothed, at least in Mama's mind—and apparently yours. She must seize her chance for happiness while I am denied any such possibility." It was not fair to Jane, but in her hurt and horror, she could only feel bitterness.

"Is there another gentleman who will take you?" he asked harshly. "Do you believe Mr Wickham, whom Mr Darcy has already ruined, will support you on an officer's pay? Perhaps you would prefer Mr Collins? Or has Mr Darcy changed his mind, and now finds you 'handsome enough to tempt him'?"

"You are cruel," Elizabeth whispered, tears burning her eyes.

He sighed, and his tone softened. "I do not mean to be. You will understand how difficult it is when you are a parent. I would see you taken care of for the rest of your life. I assure you—it is your welfare I pursue in this matter. If you find yourself a wealthy widow in twenty years, it will not be too late to seek your own happiness. Goulding is my dear friend—"

"A dear friend who has called in his markers. A dear friend to whom you sell me. A dear friend who will see our family ruined if you do not." Her voice dripped with bitter sarcasm.

"He acts for more than selfish reasons," he argued, his voice rising again. "The heir presumptive to Haye-Park is a childless, elderly cousin in ill health. The next in line after him is known for his callousness, and Goulding does not trust him. The idea of his tenants suffering, of everything he has spent his life working for going to someone unworthy—well, I, of all people, can sympathise."

"How very compassionate of you! Forgive me for thinking the price of your pity too high since it involves forcing me into a union I do not want!"

Mr Bennet stood with more force than usual. He strode across the room and retrieved a book from a side table before returning to his desk chair. "I am not interested in discussing this further. Goulding needs a wife young enough to provide him with his heir, and you require a good, loyal husband who will treat you well and provide for your future. Had my cousin Collins anything at all in his brainbox, I would have insisted one of you girls take him. As it is, I must assure him that both my eldest already have certain prospects, and he must take a second look at Mary. Perhaps the three of you may have a triple wedding and send your mother into paroxysms of planning pleasure."

How could he tease at a time like this? And the very idea of sharing a wedding with Jane, so in love with the handsome, genial Mr Bingley—while *she* was forced to marry a man older than her father—was a sick joke.

"You may also tell Mr Collins to look elsewhere for a partner for the opening set tonight," she said, doing her best not to let her voice or manner betray her growing despair. "I shall not attend."

"I will not permit you to stay at home, bemoaning your fate and wallowing in self-pity. You will go to the ball with your family. I am certain that after you give the matter due consideration, you will realise all the *personal* benefits of the match. That you will have the means to save your entire family is but an additional advantage."

Even through the turbulence in her mind, Elizabeth could feel the bitter irony of her father, for once, thinking ahead for his family's welfare.

"I shall make no announcement this evening. Not even your mother knows as yet. This night is for dancing and merriment. You may celebrate your girlhood with all the others. Your prospects were never very good, and this is an excellent match, one you will learn to appreciate. It is time to grow up, Elizabeth."

At that, he picked up his book, his usual barrier against further discussion. She would find no mercy here.

With a heavy heart, she made her way to her bedchamber to lie down and stare at the ceiling, too heart-broken even to cry.

E lizabeth readied herself for the ball as slowly as
humanly possible. Everything felt wrong—her
hands were clumsy, her limbs nerveless. Every
time she looked in the mirror, it seemed a stranger was
there, peering back at her with deadened eyes. The six
Bennet ladies, when decked in ballroom regalia, could
not all fit in the carriage at the same time regardless, and
it must return for her and Mary, who had drawn the
short straw on inclusion in the first round of the three-
mile journey.

"What is wrong with you, Lizzy?" she asked, after
walking in to find Elizabeth staring blankly at the wall
instead of donning her gown.

Elizabeth only shrugged. *I have been pierced in the
heart and am bleeding to death inside*, she thought but
could not say.

Her glance settled on the half-finished embroidery
on the bodice; she had been unable to summon an
interest in finishing it. What did it matter? Even if Mr
Wickham *did* dance with her, he would never be an

acceptable choice of husband, as her father had so unkindly pointed out. Had Mr Wickham been so lost to reason—or deceived regarding her fortune—as to ask for her hand in marriage, she would have had to refuse. Whether or not his circumstance was his own fault, he simply could not afford an impoverished wife. She knew few men who could; she ought to have been looking within the circles her uncle inhabited. She had been as blind as her father had accused Goulding of being, blind and unreasoning, believing that life might deliver her up a suitable love match as it had for Jane.

Not that her father would have approved of a husband from the less elevated circles of trade and business. He would have fought such ideas, tooth and nail.

Regardless, it was too late for should haves or could haves; the only circles remaining were in her thoughts, spinning round and round, aimless and useless in a desolate refrain of, *if only, if only, if only*.

After finally arriving at Netherfield, she quickly found a large retiring room. It was nearly empty except for two maids, waiting in readiness should their assistance be needed. Assured Elizabeth required none, they politely ignored her. She stared out of a small window at the darkening landscape below, seeing nothing.

When the room ceased to be a refuge, she knew she had better make an appearance in the ballroom. Meeting the eyes of no one was simple in the crush; instead, she cast about for Charlotte Lucas. Elizabeth needed a friend desperately.

Once she spotted Charlotte sitting and watching the dancing, however, Elizabeth's urge to speak of her unhappiness disappeared abruptly under a wave of realisation. Charlotte had longed to marry for some years. Her practical friend would look at Mr Goulding and prosperous Haye-Park and call Lizzy a fool for caring about age and choice. Nearly any sensible man who could provide a secure future would do for her.

Elizabeth quickly walked in the opposite direction, searching for some corner or nook where she might remain unobserved.

The very opposite of sensible, Mr Collins tore past her without noticing, intent upon his goal; he marched directly up to attack Mr Darcy, of all people, with introductions he had no business making. Mr Collins prefaced his speech with a solemn bow, and though she could not hear a word of it, Elizabeth saw in the motion of his lips the words 'apology', 'Hunsford', and 'Lady Catherine de Bourgh.' Mr Darcy was eyeing him with unrestrained wonder, and Elizabeth, unable to bear observing any more, moved away.

At that moment, she caught sight of her father—fortunately turned away from her, heading towards the card room. *To gamble away some other daughter*, she wondered? *Perhaps to secure another of my sisters in reserve on the chance I perform inadequately? After all, my history suggests a feminine prejudice.* Smiling bitterly, she imagined Mr Goulding in the garb of King Henry VIII, demanding her head for a failure to produce male offspring.

Continuing to avoid anyone who knew her well, Elizabeth at last discovered an empty alcove where she might watch the dancing in peace. Unfortunately, her feelings were too raw, too hurt, and when Mr Bingley and Jane promenaded up the centre together between two lines of dancers, both smiling in obvious elation, she had to turn away.

I am happy for my sister. *I would not see her suffer as I do.*

Nevertheless, it was too hard to remain an isolated spectator to Jane's rosy future, a happiness Elizabeth was unlikely to know unless she could find a way to avoid marrying Mr Goulding without it destroying her family. If she could not, contentment was the best she could hope for—should she produce a male child. If she bore only daughters, as her mother had, or no children at all, she would face the resentment of a spouse who would hate her, ruining even that pale ambition.

Four and twenty hours ago, all her hopes would have been answered by a dance with Mr Wickham; at present, she could not imagine dancing with anyone.

Somewhat blindly, she made for the large double doors leading to the terrace; despite the chill of the November evening, perhaps she could hide there until the first of her neighbours departed. She might beg them to return her to Longbourn.

Unfortunately, several others had escaped the ballroom's heat, and the terrace was almost crowded. The garden seemed to be the only place of retreat remaining.

Elizabeth had barely pierced the shadows edging the garden's entry, when she found herself suddenly addressed by none other than Mr Darcy.

"Oh!" she gasped. "How you startled me!"

"It is an odd time to view the gardens, especially lacking a warmer garment," he said in his usual sober tones. "Far be it from me to suspend any pleasure of yours, however. May I accompany you?"

This application took her so much by surprise that she accepted without knowing what she did.

Why am I such a simpleton? she thought. *Could I not think of some excuse to avoid his gallantry?*

"Would you take my coat, were I to offer it to you?" he asked.

"I would not," she replied. "If there is any chill, I do not feel it."

They strolled along the lamplit paths without speaking a word. She was glad to believe their silence would last through the night; fancifully, she pictured him as only part of the surrounding darkness, losing herself again in her morbid thoughts.

It was almost startling to hear his voice finally split the night. "I daresay the ball is an agreeable one, should you care to return to the dancing."

Her resentment produced a caustic answer. "Heaven forbid! That would be the greatest misfortune of all! To find a ball agreeable which one is determined to hate! Do not wish me such an evil, but please, feel free to discover your own joy in it."

Their silence resumed as though it had never been broken. Why did Mr Darcy not return to the party? It was politeness, she supposed. She wanted only one thing in this world, and that was to be left alone. After several minutes, it occurred to her that if she tortured him enough by obliging him to speak, he might leave her to her misery.

"It is your turn to say something now, sir. I expressed my opinion of the ball, and you ought to make some kind of remark on the size of the garden, or the number of couples avoiding its beauties."

"How foolish to allow a slight November nip in the air to keep one confined to a ballroom. Shall I comment upon the shadowy silhouette of Bingley's shrubberies? Or the relative size of the garden's bench, which appears just wide enough for two to sit and gaze at the blackness —or bleakness—surrounding them."

She was very nearly roused from her apathy by her astonishment at his words—there was wit in them, perhaps even an acknowledgement of the desolation impelling her into a cold garden obscured by night. With a lift of her brow, she noticed the bench he named and, with a shrug of her shoulders, made her way to it and sat.

The silence lingered. Mr Darcy was, perhaps, slightly better company than she had expected—or at least, she must admit, a little more astute. Then again, Mr Wickham had never claimed him to be stupid. Besides, Mr Wickham, with his troubles concerning Mr Darcy, belonged to another world—a world wherein one might take an interest in the doings of their neighbours, in their flaws and foibles, dreams and dramas. There was no room in her listless heart for sketching the character of either gentleman.

"Very well," she replied, with only a trace of her old spirit. "That reply will do for the present. Perhaps, by and by, I may observe that private gardens are much pleasanter than public ones, but now we may be silent."

The air was cold, and her dress was designed for a heated ballroom, but she was numb to such inconveniences. She had no desire to converse, think, or even be aware of Mr Darcy—or anyone else. Her mind instead tried to design some plan or scheme to thwart her father's wishes. Yet how could she allow her family to be wholly ruined? It was one thing to fight for her own happiness; it was quite another to be the only means of securing her mother and sisters' future welfare. She could probably bargain for time in exchange for docility. But what good would time do her other than give her endless hours to think, to develop her disgust, her terror, even, of the future? And yet, to face such a marriage so quickly, it was impossible to contemplate! Looking up at the unusually clear night sky, she saw the gleam of a perfect moon with some disbelief—how could the heavens retain their beauty when life had become such an ugly, untenable thing?

"Miss Elizabeth, what is the matter?" Mr Darcy suddenly asked with a greater feeling than she had ever heard from him, his voice startling her from her reverie.

"Let me call your mother. Is there nothing you could take to give you present relief? A glass of wine—shall I get you one? You are very upset."

She stared at him blankly as he held out a handkerchief, only then realising that tears fell down her cheeks, dripping off her chin and onto her bodice, leaving spots that would stain the delicate fabric.

He shrugged out of his jacket and draped it around her shoulders. "You must take my coat—you are chilled. It is much too cold out here. I ought not to have brought you so far into the garden, where the walls do not protect from the night breezes."

"No, I mean, I thank you," she replied, endeavouring to recover herself. "There is nothing the matter with me. I am quite well."

"Oh, certainly you are," he said with a touch of sharpness. "Whom can I bring you? Miss Bennet?"

"No!" she cried, with some acid of her own. "No one!"

He continued staring at her with—she realised—a mixture of distress and compassion. *What does it matter whether I explain, to this near stranger, the news which has brought me low? I must become accustomed to the telling of it. Why not practise on the one man in the county who disapproves of me and despises my family? If nothing else, he will, finally, leave me alone.*

After all, her dignity was already as ruined as her new dress.

"You are to congratulate me, Mr Darcy. I have just discovered—this very day, in fact—that I am to be married." Her voice wobbled, but she gained control once more. "One of my father's friends—a man of fortune and property—has offered for me, and Papa has-has accepted on my behalf."

She managed the announcement well enough, she thought. Unfortunately, and to her utter dismay, she then burst into noisy tears. It was all she could do, as the grief tore from her, to silence her sobs, cover her face, and try and curl into a ball, wishing he would leave and she could disappear.

But he did not. After a few moments, Elizabeth felt his heavy hand upon her shaking shoulders, straightening his coat to better cover her—and then remaining there, a compassionate weight. He said nothing, thankfully, until her sobs were reduced to hiccoughs. The handkerchief he gave to her was soon soaked with her tears.

"I am grieved for you," he said finally, his voice low and gentle.

Elizabeth took a shuddering breath. "I am a fool to care, I suppose. I-I had always believed the choice would be my own and never prepared myself for a different fate. In a prudential light, it is a very good match for me. Our estate is entailed—to my cousin, Mr Collins, who introduced himself to you this evening so rudely. I suppose it could be worse...Papa might have betrothed me to *him*." She tried for a weak smile, but it would not emerge.

"He is not the first man to introduce himself to me at a party. Think nothing of it," Mr Darcy said kindly.

Mr Darcy...kind? It was a strange notion, but she could think of nothing to say in reply.

At long last, he ventured another remark. "We live in modern times. Your father cannot force you to speak vows, not according to the law."

She nearly bit out a sarcasm, for should the head of her home refuse to feed her if she refused to wed, or... well, there were a hundred ways to force a powerless female's hand. But Mr Darcy was well enough acquainted with Mr Bennet; he would know such obvious cruelty was not part of her father's nature.

"There is another circumstance," she found herself admitting. "It was not within my father's ability to refuse the suit." Even now, furious with Papa for gambling or borrowing that which he could not repay, and mourning that he would use her to extract himself from the obligation, she would not shame him.

Mr Darcy made no reply and they simply sat, music wafting faintly from the open doors of the ballroom while her thoughts careened wildly within her head. She did not note the time, but she thought a full set had come and gone; her posterior was numb from sitting. His hand remained upon her back, unmoving, more as though he feared she would topple over than anything else. She was nearly chilled through, even with his evening coat, and realised he must be freezing.

She sighed. "I would not have anyone question your absence. You must have been long desiring to return to the ballroom."

With her words, she stood; he did as well. Her knees

trembled as her balance wavered, but she made herself hand him back the jacket. "I thank you for your coat and your sympathy. My gratitude would be complete if you could contrive to forget this entire incident, along with my unsociable, taciturn disposition." This time, she forced a false smile onto her face.

He did not return it.

"When is the wedding to take place?" he asked.

"I was...not in the mood to agree to set a date this afternoon," she replied. "Just a few minutes ago, I was contemplating a trade of compliance for a long betrothal. Yet the bridegroom is not a young man, and I believe he is impatient to see it done. I do not suppose I can hold out for a year, whatever I might wish."

Mr Darcy nodded. "Will you go back indoors now?"

She shook her head. "Neither my dress nor my face is acceptable for company any longer. I shall wait in the conservatory or another out-of-the-way spot until my parents are ready to leave."

"Go around to the front of the house. Within ten minutes, one of Bingley's carriages will be there to return you to Longbourn."

"Oh, I cannot ask you to—"

"You did not ask it of me," he replied with some urgency. "Please, allow me to perform this one small service. I shall contrive to inform your parents that you were taken home with the excuse of a headache from the overheated ballroom. If you agree, they shall be assured that the Bingleys would not hear of disrupting their enjoyment of the evening."

Elizabeth nodded with some relief. The ball would probably continue until the small hours of the morning, and she was already exhausted; when her father learnt of the weak excuse, he might be irritated, but her mother would think it a further sign of Mr Bingley's favour. There would be no repercussions. "It is very kind of you."

They turned together, walking towards the brightly lit home, saying nothing. As they drew closer, she could see several people standing about the terrace; she halted before they emerged from the shadows.

"I shall slip around the side, so we are not noticed together. We would not wish for incorrect conclusions to be drawn."

He looked at her a little oddly, she thought, but she strode swiftly away, making for the path that would, eventually, lead to the drive.

In the moonlight, she easily found her way to the front of the massive home. There were a few others on the lawns and standing about—probably most were servants awaiting their merrymaking employers. In the distance, lines of coaches were parked along the lane, some with men who must be their drivers loitering nearby. No one paid her any heed.

After several minutes, an unfamiliar, smart-looking vehicle pulled up the drive from the direction of the stables. It was not the Bingley carriage, and she approached it tentatively.

"Miss Bennet?" A liveried footman let down the steps and opened the door.

"Yes, thank you," she said as she stepped in, folding herself gratefully into the comfortable interior, smoothing a hand over the luxuriously upholstered seat. Was this Mr Darcy's own carriage? The door closed behind her, and they jolted forward.

"What a strange evening," she said aloud to herself. She had spent a silent half an hour with Mr Darcy once before, in the Netherfield library, when she and Jane stayed at the estate. Elizabeth had thought it the oddest thing in the world that he made no acknowledgement of her presence there. Perhaps in a home or a ballroom, it was rather odd. Tonight, she had discovered that when one was in mourning—and she *was*, mourning for a life for which she might no longer even hope, for choices she could no longer make—a mostly silent companion was a good deal more desirable than one who recited blessings one was loath to count or gave encouragement one was in no mood to hear. Mr Darcy had been, she realised, just the sort of friend she needed.

With a little start of surprise, she recalled how, earlier this very day, she had wished to confront Mr Darcy regarding his injustice to Mr Wickham. It felt like that was another Elizabeth, so profoundly had her father's demands altered her. She *might* have even taunted Mr Darcy with his sins—pretending cleverness while truthfully only wishing to satisfy her own curiosity. However, their interlude together allowed her to recognise in him a deeply bred *civility*, for lack of a better word. Whatever the troubled history between those two men, she was no judge of it. Besides, curiosity had been burnt from her like a spent coal.

Leaning back into the softly padded cushions, she turned her thoughts to the future, wondering how she could possibly change it.

Three

Two days after the ball, Elizabeth found herself tramping between Netherfield and Longbourn. Her own house was in too much of an uproar to bear, and she sought the privacy and pleasure only nature could provide. Her attempt that morning to discuss with her father other avenues of rescuing their home and his honour had devolved into furious ultimatums; in the end, she felt fortunate that they had reached an uneasy truce with his agreement that she would be given time to adjust to the situation. The duration of such a reprieve was undetermined. Would it be long enough for her to think of some other way, though? She very much feared even several years would be too short an interlude.

She was startled when Mr Darcy appeared before her, for the weather was uncertain, and she was just as far from Netherfield as from Longbourn.

"Mr Darcy!" she said stupidly.

He seemed taken aback on finding her alone and greeted her soberly.

"This is a favourite path of mine," she informed him,

in case he wished to avoid encountering her in the future.

"You are at least better prepared for the out of doors today," he said approvingly, instead of commenting on her lack of accompanying maid, as she might once have expected from such a proper gentleman.

She wore her oldest, heaviest coat, and her black umbrella was hooked over her arm. "I was hoping you would forget our last meeting." She blushed at the recollection. "I thank you for prevailing upon Mrs Hurst to present my excuses regarding my early departure from the ball. Mama could only speak well of her solicitousness."

He shook his head dismissively. "How do you fare?"

Sighing, she began walking again, too restless to stand still, leaving him to follow if he wished. It was possible he only asked out of politeness, but her thoughts were too full of that morning's row to prevaricate. "Papa and I are at a draw, for now. In exchange for his unwilling silence and delay, he gains my unwilling obedience. However, I feel we are bound to disappoint each other. I do not know whether I have three weeks or three months before he presses for the betrothal, but I cannot imagine much more than the latter."

Mr Darcy had fallen into step beside her, shortening his pace to match her own. He did not respond to her explanation. Suddenly, she wished for nothing more than to break into a run and never stop. She did her best not to resent Mr Darcy's presence, for it was not his fault she was in no mood for company; had he tried to engage her in conversation, she might have even tried sprinting away. But he was his usual taciturn self, and once again, after several moments, she managed to forget him.

Well, that was not quite true; he was too large, too outsized a presence to forget. However, she was not required to chat, entertain, charm, or divert; in other words, he asked nothing of her presence except to allow his own. It was a kindness, as it had been the night of the ball.

After walking some time in complete silence, he broke it. "How do your sisters do?" he asked politely.

She glanced at him, and almost to her own surprise, found herself telling him. "Mr Collins proposed marriage to my sister Mary yesterday."

He lifted a brow. "Are congratulations in order?"

For the first time in two days, a ghost of a smile touched her lips. "I really cannot say."

His head crooked a bit towards her in unspoken enquiry.

"He proposed to her while they ate breakfast. Mama, Lydia, Kitty, and I were in the next room, with both doors open. We could hear every word. He carefully explained to her all the reasons he had decided to marry, including Lady Catherine de Bourgh's insistence that he take a wife and that Mary's home must belong to him one day when her father is dead. He promised to generously overlook her impoverishment and, finally, claimed he was overcome with violent affection for her."

"Indeed." His expression was unmoved, but there

was a slight sign of...something. It was possibly humour, but probably only incredulity.

"Mary instantly thanked him for the compliment of his offer but assured him she could not accept. With that, I thought the matter was done."

"It was not?"

"No. He claimed it was a usual practise for young ladies to reject the addresses of a man whom they secretly meant to accept when he first applied for their favour. Further, sometimes the refusal is repeated a second or even a third time. He was, therefore, by no means discouraged."

"How did your sister respond to this, um, lack of discouragement?"

Elizabeth shook her head. "She did not. To the best of our hearing, they both continued with their meal. At one point, she asked him whether she could refill his cup. At another, he offered to cut her viands into a more manageable portion for the delicacy of her lips."

"Indeed," he repeated, in tones of some wonder.

"I cannot decide whether it was a ruse upon Mary's part, allowing him to think himself successfully engaged without actually committing herself, or whether she truly wishes for him to propose two or three times yet in the future."

"Once he is no longer a guest in your home, she could have her father present her refusals," he noted. "It might be less awkward for her."

"Only if she is prepared to have her lips, and any

other delicacies, complimented unceasingly until he leaves."

"Some ladies enjoy compliments."

"I think every lady must enjoy a sincere one. However, endless homage uttered for the sake of admiring one's own voice? I cannot think of anything less appealing."

They walked for several moments before she realised Mr Darcy would give no reply because there was nothing courteous he could think to say.

From the moment she had met Mr Collins, and even since she read his first letter, Elizabeth's opinion had been that such a preposterous nature deserved any mockery it provoked.

I copy my father's behaviour in that, she thought, suddenly ashamed of her manners, if not the sentiment behind them. She had always enjoyed the thought that she was similar to her father; it was lowering to find it no longer an ideal to be proud of.

On the heels of these thoughts, a new one occurred to her. She perfectly remembered everything that had passed between Mr Wickham and herself their first evening together at Mr and Mrs Philips's home. She was struck by the impropriety of such communications to a stranger and wondered it had escaped her before. She saw the indelicacy of putting himself forward as he had done, and the inconsistency of his professions with his actions. In comparison, Mr Darcy seemed always to conduct himself with refinement.

She glanced at her once-again silent companion, her

brow furrowing as she questioned Mr Wickham's version of their history.

"Did Mr Wickham attend Mr Bingley's ball?" she asked, before she could think too much about it.

The effect was immediate. A deeper shade of something—hauteur? anger? resentment?—overspread his features, but he said not a word, and Elizabeth regretted asking.

At length, however, Mr Darcy spoke and in a constrained tone, said, "He did not. Mr Wickham is blessed with such happy manners as may ensure his making friends—but neither Bingley nor myself is amongst them."

"Why, Mr Darcy! How awful a man he must be, to have earned such disparagement!" Elizabeth heard the tease escape from her own lips and was rather astonished by it. Such behaviour seemed to belong to the 'old' version of herself.

He looked at her in surprise and then, somewhat sheepishly, said, "I have reason to believe you, of all people, know that I am no saint, especially when it comes to opening my mouth when it would be much better shut."

It took her a moment to understand him. But of course, she did know. With everything that had happened lately, his insult the night they first met had faded into insignificance. "I suppose I ought not to have repeated what you said at the assembly, words I imagine you spoke thoughtlessly. I am no saint either, it seems."

"Any scorn I face is deserved."

She ought not to be surprised by his sentiments, but she acknowledged that, except for the night of the ball, she had looked to him only to find fault.

Another of Papa's bad habits. It is past time to forget that stupid insult. I have far more important matters with which to occupy my thoughts.

"Miss Bingley believes I am remiss in my duty," he said, in what seemed to her an abrupt change of topic. "She believes her brother is in danger. Is he?"

"I am afraid I do not understand your question, sir. In danger of what?"

"I had not been long in Hertfordshire, before I saw, in common with others, that Bingley prefers your eldest sister to any other young woman in the country. I have often seen him in love before, but Miss Bingley believes he has behaved in such a way as to create a general expectation of marriage. Has he?" His tone had grown harsher, as if the very idea were repugnant.

She had been enjoying his company too well, and though she knew it to be foolish, was hurt by his sudden return to severity. "What if he has?" she asked sharply. "Jane is not committed to another. Is *he*? Her birth is better than his, and even though she has no fortune, any man would be privileged to win her regard!"

He stiffened and, if possible, grew even more formal. "Bingley's partiality for her is beyond what I have ever witnessed in *him*. I have observed Miss Bennet closely of late. Her look and manners are open, cheerful, and engaging, but without any symptom of peculiar regard. I am left to wonder whether she returns his sentiments. It is plain your mother wishes for the match, but does your sister? Has her heart been touched? In my opinion, it has not. It might be rude of me to ask, but Bingley relies on my guidance. My inclination is to advise him to instantly show the world it was nothing beyond an acquaintance, perhaps even departing the area and giving up the lease. I have not been pleased with the condition of Netherfield in many respects, which was misrepresented to me when I sought to help him lease a property."

Elizabeth's mouth gaped open in astonishment. "You would rely on your observations to determine what my sister, whom you have known scarcely more than a month, feels? Is her future happiness, and that of your friend, to be decided by you because, in your judgment, she does not *look* like she is in love with him? Tell me, Mr Darcy, what must a woman do to show she cares for a gentleman? How would you know if a lady feels affection for *you*?"

A certain sadness had crept into her tone; just when she had begun to think better of him, her opinion abruptly sank. She would not let him see it, however, and covered those feelings with a rising anger.

"I suppose Jane could compliment Mr Bingley's penmanship, his letters, or at least the speed with which he writes them," she cried. "Perhaps she should note his fine figure as he strolls about a room? Or add a few indirect boasts, whereby he might particularly notice her most worthwhile qualities?" Elizabeth shook her head. "But no, these are the means by which others call attention to their feelings—not Jane, the refined, genteel Jane, who strives, even when very much in love, to be an example all of her sisters might be pleased to follow.

"If you expected flirtation instead of sincerity or flattery instead of graciousness, you would miss any sign of her feelings she is ever likely to give. But then, *she* is thoughtful and good-natured. No wonder *you* could not see them." Elizabeth looked at him unflinchingly, her chest heaving with anger.

He stared back, astonishment visible upon his face.

With a sickening rush, she realised she had done Jane no favours today. With Herculean effort, she grappled with her temper and leashed it.

"I apologise, Mr Darcy," she forced the words out from behind the lump in her throat. "I ask you not to blame my kind and gentle sister for my unruly tongue. My feelings have been too troubled of late for other reasons, and I have forgotten myself. Pray forgive me." After the briefest of curtseys, she fled at the fastest pace she could manage without breaking into a run. She felt his eyes burning into her back until the woods closed behind her

Four

Elizabeth did not expect to see Mr Darcy on her next ramble two days later. She had told him that she walked this particular path frequently, specifically so that he could avoid meeting her. After their last encounter, nay, their last *two* encounters, he must doubtlessly have no desire *ever* to see her. Even so, she was curious and could not prevent a desire to talk to him again.

She had missed an opportunity yesterday, when Mr Darcy had come to Longbourn in company with Mr Bingley. She and Kitty had not been home, having been sent on an errand to Meryton by her mother with fabrics for Mrs Philips. Elizabeth gladly volunteered for such duties now, welcoming any useful distraction, even listening to her aunt and Kitty exchange the dullest sort of gossip on the minutiae of their neighbours' lives.

Elizabeth had wondered whether she would see Mr Wickham in town; she no longer hoped for it. Doubts had risen within her about him, regardless of her feelings for Mr Darcy—those feelings a confusing mixture, to be sure, of interest and resentment braided together like a rug in baffling patterns. Sometimes one shade dominated, colouring her entire view in antipathy; infused within the design, however, were silky threads of awareness, even of appeal.

She had repeated their conversation again and again in her mind. Yes, she had not much cared for his tone, which had seemed to imply distaste for a match between Mr Bingley and her sister; and she had taken umbrage at his idea that his friend ought to leave the area. However, she had ignored entirely one key element of Mr Darcy's conversation: he had *asked her opinion*.

It had been an opportunity for her to show him, by word and manner, that not all the Bennets were uncivil; she might have simply and mildly answered his question by hinting delicately at Jane's feelings rather than boldly naming them and, in essence, calling him a brute. The worst part was, Elizabeth did not know whether she was most upset on Jane's behalf or her own. Somehow, without knowing quite how it happened, she had come to value his opinion *of her*.

Those regrets did not matter, of course. She was the next thing to betrothed, and he knew it. Besides, Mr Darcy would never have any interest in an impoverished bride without connexion or influence within his elevated sphere.

Why was she even wasting her time on these thoughts? Her own future was decided; encouraging the fancies of handsome, solemn men before whom one was inclined to make a fool of oneself was the worst type of distraction and would only lead to bitter disappointment.

After her display of temper, Elizabeth had been certain that the next she would hear of Mr Darcy would be from the gossips, informing them of the Netherfield party's departure from the area. Instead, Jane had been practically floating, her eyes sparkling with delight and day-dreams when Elizabeth returned home from her errand. Mr Bingley had accepted a dinner invitation for Monday evening; it seemed clear that he, his family, and friend were remaining in the neighbourhood, and his courtship was proceeding unimpeded by Miss Bingley's or Mr Darcy's objections or disfavour.

As though her thoughts had conjured him, Mr Darcy appeared on the path.

Elizabeth, amidst confusion and regrets, experienced an unusual attack of shyness, not knowing what to say. Fortunately, as was usual with him, conversation proved unnecessary. He merely bowed, which she answered with a curtsey, and began to walk beside her with hardly an interruption to her pace.

She was acutely aware of him today, less able to relegate him to the background of her thoughts—and not only because she had spoken so imprudently at their last conversation. So be it. There were things she should say to him before she lost her courage.

"I would like to thank you," she said quietly.

He peered at her with one brow raised.

"I have been—since receiving notice of my own impending nuptials—very angry at Jane."

"Oh?" His tone held a note of surprise, and she could not blame him after her impassioned defence of her sister. In truth, she had been shocked when she understood her feelings.

"Why should Jane be allowed to experience great happiness, to have her dreams come true, while I am forced to surrender all of mine? I am a selfish creature, you see. If *I* cannot be happy, why should a most beloved sister?"

"I do not think it selfish. It is a very natural response, I would say."

She shrugged a little. "Natural, perhaps, but still selfish. When I—there is no other way to describe it—lost my temper with you, it cleared the barrier I had unknowingly erected between myself and my love for Jane. I *do* wish her to be happy, of course I do. If she were miserable too, it would double my burden, not halve it. You have made me see how unworthy my thoughts have been. By your intervention, I was properly humbled."

He shook his head—in disagreement, or perhaps confusion. "You were right in what you said to me." His voice was low and deep, warm and comforting. "I do not know your sister. I should not have assumed a few hours of observation meant I understood her heart."

"Charlotte once warned Jane that she was doing too fine a job of keeping her feelings concealed. My family is not generally known for our soberness of manner, and the contrast with how she acts...I can understand why you would worry, given how free my mother has been about her wish for Mr Bingley to offer for Jane and what you know of my father's willingness to force me into a match I do not want. I would not blame you for thinking we are all grasping and shallow."

He stopped in the path, lightly touching her arm until she looked at him. "I do not think that, would never think it, of you or Miss Bennet."

Elizabeth acknowledged his assurances with a fleeting smile. She knew her youngest sisters often behaved wild, and her parents did little to check them. At least, in missing the greatest part of the ball, she had likely avoided witnessing her family exposing the worst of their defects to all and sundry.

"Ah, but in reward for my attempts to conduct myself with propriety, I have won the prize—my father's friend has said he would only take Jane or me. Jane is to be left free to entertain hopes of Mr Bingley." Elizabeth chuckled, although it was without humour. "I believe I have been mistaken in my life choices. I ought to have been making a fool of myself with the officers and overindulging at the punch bowl!"

She had expected him to smile, and yet he did not.

"Who is your suitor?"

"I have no suitor," she said. "Only an old man who requires a convenient wife to bear him a convenient heir." She turned away. "If you will forgive me, I truly do *not* wish to speak of him today. Will the sun, do you think, be willing to peek out from yonder clouds this afternoon?"

It was a clumsy conversational shift, but mercifully, he dropped the subject. They resumed walking, and she cast about for something to say, since he showed no inclination to pursue the topic of weather. Nothing much came to mind. The wind blew colder as she took the path rising upwards and encircling Oakham Mount. Mr Darcy did not question the change in direction, although the climb was somewhat steep. Had her hat not been securely pinned, it might have blown away in the stiffening breeze.

"I always loved the view from here," she said at last, looking out from a stone outcropping at the peak of the escarpment. It was a sharp drop, but she had no fear of heights. To her left, she could see Longbourn's smoking chimneys; to her right, Netherfield stood in all its stone glory as it had for the last hundred years, ruling over their little valley. "I had hoped I could love it still."

"Can you not?"

Instead of answering immediately, she stepped back and turned towards a large boulder propped a little lower down on the hillside. It offered some protection from the wind, and she sat upon its lip. The vista was still on display, if not quite so dramatically. Mr Darcy rested one booted foot upon the same boulder, draping his arm casually over his knee.

"I shall tell you my little secret," she confided. "I am working on a venture—a great one, and all the greater because I do not *wish* to do it. I have begun counting my blessings."

He glanced at her with, she thought, a slight interest. Or perhaps it was only politeness. His response, however, showed perception.

"You feel this undertaking a risk?" he asked.

"Yes. Do not the sermons promise such tallying is the antidote for unhappiness? Yet, it is easiest to see only the blessings I have been denied. I long to shake my fist at heaven and demand a different fate. I wish to cling to my feelings, my anger, which seems true and right to me. What if I surrender them, only to find I have been disregarded entirely, everything important to me, about me, overlooked and ignored? Thus, it is a '*Great* Project'—to be pronounced with capital letters. I have challenged myself to find one thing each day for which I genuinely feel grateful—even if it is only by the tiniest morsel. Perhaps nothing can outweigh the bitter burdens of resentment, but I can slip something else onto the scales."

"Am I to understand that your present gratitude is for the view from this hill?"

His question was conveyed in all seriousness. He had not said she was being ridiculous; Elizabeth could only imagine the mockery such a confession would produce from her father. Instead, Mr Darcy seemed to be attempting that rarest of all enterprises—trying to *understand*.

"Not at all." She returned her attention to the view, wishing she could answer in the positive. "I cannot feel anything about it. It may as well be painted in shades of grey."

"I see. Then are your thanks for Miss Bennet's situation?"

"Oh, no. That was yesterday's blessing. I still

possess a determined wish for Jane's happiness, even though I cannot feel particularly drenched in appreciation for it today. But I have the...the residue of it. In a thousand days, I shall have the collective gratitude of a thousand memories. One small brick at a time will surely build me a mighty structure. I have not discovered what today's will be. I had hoped I would see it from this vantage point, but the search proves stubborn."

"Ah."

"At least I have made a beginning," she said, hearing the doubt in his tone. It was also in her own.

Together they looked out over the valley floor, the roiling clouds failing to prevent a rather splendid ray of sunshine from breaking through the gloom, creating a vivid prospect. Mr Darcy pointed it out as a striking possibility for appreciation.

"I suppose the fact that one has food to eat, shelter from ill weather, and warm clothes upon one's back are all excellent reasons to be thankful in the strictest sense," she replied seriously. "But I have discovered there is nothing designed to ruin one's best intentions more quickly than having others help with the count. I *know* what I *should* feel. It matters not at all. I cannot feel it, and lectures on the *shoulds* make everything worse."

"I withdraw the suggestion," he said immediately. "The scene before us features nothing more brilliant than a dingy prospect accentuating the dullness of the landscape."

"Your retraction is accepted," Elizabeth said grandly,

as though she were the queen, and found a half-hearted smile to go with it.

She took a deep breath, trying her best to fix upon optimism rather than sorrow. The air smelt of coming rain, of wet earth, of greenery. Between the scent and the surrounding nature, she felt, at last, the barest wisp of the peace she sought. Mr Darcy's presence—or, to be fair, her temper—had not ruined it, unlike the last time they walked together.

"In truth, I did not actually believe I would find something to appreciate up here. It was only to view the horizon," she said at last. "In the past, when things at Longbourn seemed particularly discouraging, I would ascend this path to force myself to look further ahead. My aunt Gardiner has long intended that she and my uncle will take a northern tour, and she has hinted they might bring me with them. Most recently, I have climbed Oakham Mount while trying to envision travelling, and seeing parts of England I have only read about. Things I cannot do yet, but which might be a cause for hope in the future."

"Hope on the horizon," he said.

"Exactly."

"Have you found it?"

"I am not certain, but I found *something*. I do not believe my present grief can last. I was not formed for unhappiness. I cannot live with fury and resentment eating away at me. I do not know what will break its hold upon me, but I am determined to look, even though it seems improbable to expect my new husband to grant me permission to leave on a northern tour with my relations from Cheapside."

A scowl formed on his brow. Was it dismay or distaste at the mention of her relations in trade? She could not tell. Mr Darcy was expert at keeping his thoughts to himself.

"The Peak District is beautiful," he said, moving to sit beside her on the boulder. "If I were an artist, I think all my subjects would be attempts at capturing its endless views. Alas, I lack both artistic talent and the vocabulary for adequate description."

It was an obvious bid to talk about something else, which Elizabeth did with some relief. "Oh, I remember now that your estate is in Derbyshire. Will you tell me about it?"

This was a topic upon which he spoke easily, and they sat, chatting almost comfortably. She was still a bit too aware of him; he was not quite a friend, yet he knew too much about her to be considered merely an acquaintance. Did he *want* her friendship? It was impossible to know.

"How does Miss Mary do?" he asked on the return journey, the shelter of the trees blocking the chill—and much of the daylight. Elizabeth had to pay attention to her footing, lest she trip over a root in the shadows.

"Mr Collins has announced his departure for tomorrow," she replied. "His flock, he asserts, requires his return."

"He is to be disappointed then?"

"I still do not know. When he made the announcement, I thought that he was, but after breakfast, Mary suggested that she show him the hermitage. They were out of doors for some time and I assume he repeated his proposal. Before I learnt her answer, I decided to escape on a walk of my own."

"What is your preferred outcome?"

"I-I really cannot say. I cannot imagine anyone finding satisfaction in marriage to such a man. I care for my sister and wish her happy. I find it difficult to like or respect him—he is repugnant, self-important, and toadying. At the same time, I do not want my mother ever removed from her home." She paused a moment before adding, "Perhaps I have misjudged him."

"He seems exactly as you say."

She made an indifferent sound. "When we do not know a person well, or when they behave in unexpected, uncomfortable, or unusual ways, we tend to make assumptions to complete our sketches of them using our past experiences."

"As I did with your sister, you mean."

Elizabeth glanced at him, and thought she saw a hint of a smile play at his lips. "We all do it," she hastened to assure him. "When my father met my mother, he was entranced by her looks, her laughter, and her liveliness. In the brief time he took to court her, he created his own judgment of her nature. Whatever he did not know of her, he unconsciously invented—based upon nothing but who he wished her to be. I think he might not have been so disappointed had not his expectations been so dreadfully inaccurate."

Mr Darcy nodded. Was she too frank regarding her family's foibles? She quickly decided that it mattered not at all, deliberately turning her thoughts and observations in a different direction. Unbidden, they went to him— the strength and breadth of his arms and shoulders, the unconscious grace in his bearing, the way he instinctively reached for her elbow to steady her on the uneven path. They were nearly to Longbourn's borders before he spoke again.

"I did it, as well," he said, and it took her several seconds to remember what they had been discussing. She looked at him questioningly.

"When I arrived at Netherfield, I, too, unconsciously invented a character for the neighbourhood. I met Sir William Lucas and his sons, and found them lacking in reason. There were two or three other people I found equally insensible. I easily applied the same judgment— expectation, if you will—to all the rest. I am ashamed to admit it included you, at least at the assembly. I apologise."

She found a hint of amusement in the recollection. "You must not do so—after all, I have already admitted to taking my revenge in ensuring your misjudgement was repeated. I am generally well-liked, you see."

"You are harsh but fair," he nodded.

Did she, again, detect humour in his expression? *Did* he find her amusing?

She abruptly grew impatient with herself; she must not yearn for his approval. "Although, whether or not the lot of us hated you could mean nothing to a personage such as yourself."

They had come to a fence stile at the edge of Netherfield's boundary; on the other side was the path leading to Longbourn. Mr Darcy stopped before it, turning to look at her, just look, his expression grave.

"It is your turn to be the guilty party."

"Me? How have *I* misjudged *you*?" she asked with some surprise.

Instead of answering, he leant against the stile. "Did you have any success during our ramble? Have you found your one good thing for the day?"

She considered. "I believe I have."

"What is it, if I might enquire?"

Was there a hint of anticipation in his look? Unlikely, unless he was anticipating a return to the warm fires of Netherfield.

"Trees," she said.

"Trees?"

"Yes," she replied, rather enjoying his look of confusion. "I have wandered through half the forest blanketing the property between Netherfield and Longbourn. Many of these trees have stood for decades, even centuries. My little problems would mean nothing to an ancient oak, my brief life a mere collection of rings lost within so many others. I find something comforting in that."

He held her gaze for a long moment before counting off on his fingers, "Your sister. Trees. You have but nine-hundred-ninety-eight to go."

She breathed a short huff of what once might have been laughter. "You have changed the subject. I must know—how have I misjudged you?"

With a sudden movement, he lifted her in his arms and over the stile, setting her securely upon the ground on the other side.

"Oh!" she cried out.

She caught it again, a smile so brief it was gone nearly before it registered. The lift had taken him almost no effort whatsoever.

Heavens but he was strong!

"Good day, Miss Elizabeth," he said softly, bowing.

"Good day, Mr Darcy," she replied, still flustered, returning his gesture with a curtsey.

He turned on his heel and strode back in the direction of Netherfield. She watched him go, puzzled, perplexed, and perturbed by both the question he had left unanswered, and his means of avoiding it.

Five

Monday morning dawned, bringing with it the happy thought that it was the last day Elizabeth would have to watch Mr Collins plough through the breakfast offerings as though he would never see food again. After watching as he stacked enough kippers on a slice of toast to sink the British fleet, she collected her coat, slipped out of the house, through the kitchen garden plot, and hence to freedom. Mrs Bennet intended a grand send-off for the vicar, possibly shoving poor Mary into the carriage with him. Elizabeth wanted no part of what was likely to be a dramatic farewell.

It was going to snow, she surmised, and she wondered whether her coat was warm enough, even with the scarf she had wrapped around her shoulders. The cold would not prevent her escape from Longbourn, regardless. After leaving Mr Darcy yesterday, a plot had begun to form in her mind, if not to thwart her father utterly, at least to cause significant delays. Why not write to her aunt, confess the betrothal scheme, and beg for a visit? Once in Mr Gardiner's home, surely her uncle would argue on her behalf, help her father see reason. She was not asking to live with him or that he overrule Mr Bennet, only that her father's edict change into a conversation, a discussion in which she had some say.

A simple enquiry of Jane's at dinner had ruined it all.

"Did you finish your letter to Aunt Gardiner?" she had asked. "You always write such charming, long letters to her—I can never think of half so much to say."

Her father's head had turned to Elizabeth sharply, his look repressive. "Perhaps you relayed to her tales of your sister's romance and of your mother's plans for wedding bells to ring. I only hope you did not name the groom, for whether it is Mr Bingley or some other lucky fellow, we have no news to impart, do we?"

Jane had blushed and looked down at her plate, but to Elizabeth, his message had been clear:

'Put those fancies away, Elizabeth.'

If she did not marry Goulding, obedient, persuadable Jane, although deeply in love with another, must do it. She dared not even speak of it to her; Jane would sacrifice everything for her sisters.

Since that moment, Elizabeth had been possessed of a deep desire to flee Longbourn—to lose herself amongst the trees, to return to Oakham Mount, and most foolish of all, to see Mr Darcy.

I am not thinking of him—only not not thinking of him, she tried to assure herself.

She paused at the fence stile. If she took the same

path again and they met, he might believe she was seeking him out.

Why should I not? she thought defiantly. *If my life is only my own for a few short months, why should I not walk where I wish, regardless of who I might see?*

Still, she hesitated, wondering what he might think of seeing her again.

How she enjoyed talking to him! No, that was not quite it. She enjoyed *not* talking to him regarding all the things in her life upon which she did not wish to dwell. He knew of her misery, thus understood her silences. Yet, she had not always been silent, had she? She had spoken to him of pain, of coping, of hope, and of her struggle for courage. In fact, the only subject she had not mentioned was the future groom himself. *Did* that make Mr Darcy a friend of sorts?

Or, perhaps, he only provided some company in her grieving, and any reasonably astute companion would do.

And if he did not wish to *be* that companion, knowing her habits as he did, he could easily avoid the path she was about to take. This was her favourite walk, and she would not choose another simply to avoid appearing interested in a man for whom she held no interest. With a determined lift of her chin, Elizabeth crossed the stile.

The trail was a circular one, winding through wood and field. Not only was the footpath beautiful, it allowed her to remain out of sight of any tenant settlement as well as the great house.

The wind was brisk, and she kept her pace a quick one, wishing she had worn a warmer hat and brought Jane's fur muff. She wrapped the scarf more tightly around her neck. The first snowflakes materialised at the worst possible moment, exactly at the halfway mark of a long lane, with no trees to block either wind or snow. There was no point in turning back, for it would save her no time in finding shelter. The chill was growing bitter.

Mr Darcy did not appear.

You were stupid to half-anticipate him, to expect anyone *to be out of doors in this frigid, damp cold. Stupid, foolish Elizabeth!*

Genteel, refined Mr Darcy had more sense than to wander through the countryside on such a day. *How could I have imagined he would wait out here in the weather for someone such as myself?*

She had discovered something else within his absence—and it was all the more shocking, humiliating even, because she had been unaware that she would feel it.

Disappointment. *Profound* disappointment.

Did I truly think he felt anything more for me than pity, simply because he happened upon me at the most pathetic moment of my life? Hubris was the only explanation.

For she *had* thought it, or hoped it—not that he was in love with her, but that he was her friend, happily lending her strength and support during this awful time when she had no one else.

A freezing gust nipped at her, and Elizabeth

increased her already quick pace, hoping to reach the trees and escape more of the wind's rage.

Merely because he chose not to venture out during a snowstorm—which is a bit of exaggeration, but my feet are blocks of ice—does not mean much, she assured herself. He might still wish to be a friend, and a sensible one, who would stay indoors when the weather turned foul.

She was forced, then, to face another question. Had *she* gone out, ignoring the threatening clouds, largely for the purpose of seeing *him?*

She was three-quarters of the way to Longbourn's borders when she heard her name.

"Miss Elizabeth! Miss Elizabeth!"

Her heart lifted, disconnected from any restraint her will could impose. Something that felt surprisingly like giddiness swept through her in a blast stronger than the wind. It was him! He *had* come! Despair wanted to intrude on the heels of her elation, but she thrust the feeling aside. *He had come!*

Slowly she turned, as though afraid her ears had deceived her, and he would not be there.

But he was, as he had always been whenever she needed him, whether she had known it or not. He strode forward swiftly, his many-caped greatcoat emphasising the breadth of his shoulders.

"Mr Darcy," she said, her voice almost a whisper.

"Miss Elizabeth," he repeated, sounding a little breathless and bowing. "I nearly missed seeing you. I suspected you might come out, despite the weather. I lit a fire in the folly, should you require any warming."

Another wave of misery-laced joy bloomed at his consideration. "It-it s-sounds lovely." She stumbled over her words, and his look immediately changed to one of concern.

"You are chilled through," he said, frowning. "Come, let us get you indoors." Together they turned back into Netherfield's park.

He said nothing else, and she did not speak either, being too full of a confusing array of emotions, most of which she ought not to permit herself to feel.

She had no idea to which folly he referred. Netherfield had several of them, as she recalled, and she had only been inside the one nearest the lake and the Etruscan temple, which was often used as an amphitheatre for entertaining. He turned off her usual route in a south-easterly direction, cutting across a windswept field, the snow falling in thick flakes as they entered one of the many groomed paths in the vast park.

The trees were nearly impenetrable, which blocked the wind, but the temperature seemed to have dropped further. When they disturbed branches collecting snow, they were soon wearing it themselves. She shivered, hugging herself tightly, her teeth chattering. Soon, it grew difficult to force herself forward, to plant one foot in front of the other. She saw nothing resembling a building, and briefly, she wondered whether they were lost. Mr Darcy did not hesitate, however, and plunged onwards; they had to walk single file in the narrow spaces between trees. A few minutes more brought a folly into view. It resembled a miniature country house, with two chimneys and red brick exterior, complete with twin stone balconies. Elizabeth gasped at the sight of it.

"I had no idea this was even here!" she cried.

He glanced at her, his eyes crinkling just a bit at the corners. "There is no direct path leading to it. It is meant to excite wonder and astonishment in the wanderer, initiating a true spirit of discovery."

With the loss of tree cover, the snow flung itself at them with renewed purpose, collecting in the crevices and carvings of the pretty little building.

Mr Darcy took a key from his pocket and climbed the tiled steps. He opened the door wide, and Elizabeth scurried within as quickly as possible. He hung back, however.

"Come in and shut the door!" she called, going at once to a hearth where a blazing fire burned. There was a second fireplace across the room; a stack of wood sat neatly piled by each. "You will let out all the heat." She removed her hat, which was sodden, and hung it on a nearby hook, looking around with interest.

The interior was largely unfurnished. A little, curving staircase in the corner led up into the shadows. There was a polished wooden bench on one side of the room, as well as a cushioned banquette before the furthest fireplace. When she was warm enough to remove her coat and gloves, Elizabeth draped them over one end of the long bench to dry. She was about to take a seat upon the banquette when she noticed that Mr

Darcy still stood by the entrance, dripping upon the limestone floor.

In her anxious hurry to escape the cold, she had completely disregarded the decorum of entering the building and being alone with him. Why had he brought her here? The impropriety must have occurred to him when he lit the fireplaces.

"I meant to show you this place and give you the key, so you might have a private, peaceful place to come, to think, now that it has grown cold," he said. "I did not realise the weather would so quickly turn wretched."

It was probably the most thoughtful thing anyone had ever done for her. Why did she feel like crying?

Because I am an idiot, she told herself. *Of course*, he had not brought her to a cosy spot to spend time alone with her, heedless of manners or conduct. That would be a sure way to become trapped in a marriage *he* could not want. Excellent man that he was, he knew she wished to be away from Longbourn, and thus he provided a place for her. It was the charitable gesture of a *friend*. She closed her eyes briefly, then looked at him again. Boldness was her only recourse.

"Can you trust," she said, "that I would never breathe a word of this meeting or your presence here? No one will ever know we were alone. Will you stay long enough to dry your clothing, at least partly?"

His gaze and voice were both sombre. "It is I who should be promising you those very things."

She inclined her head. "I do not require your reassurances to know you would never do anything to hurt me or my reputation."

He nodded once and removed his coat and beaver, hanging them to dry on the hooks by the door. Elizabeth sat on the banquette and for a few minutes, simply enjoyed the sensation of warmth. From the corner of her eye, she noticed that Mr Darcy remained standing. It was only then she realised her wet outerwear was taking up the only other seat.

"Please, sit," she invited, scooting over to the furthest side of the banquette to ensure he had plenty of room.

After a moment, she felt the cushion shift against his weight as he sat; quick glances showed her how his wet hair curled and the shadowed growth of his beard, even though he undoubtedly had been shaved that morning. As she pretended not to watch, he loosened the limp, wet cravat, until more of his neck was visible than she had ever seen in a man unrelated to her.

It was a strong, attractive neck, and suddenly she wondered whether that curling hair would feel soft or coarse to the touch, and how the texture of his cheeks would feel beneath her caress. She flushed, forcing her attention back to the flames. And then her mouth opened and words spilled out—almost without her permission.

"Why do you allow Mr Wickham to spread lies about you?"

Six

His head jerked towards her as though he had been slapped—and she was not mistaken in the fury lighting his eyes at the mere mention of his rival. It only lasted a moment, much like the first time she had brought up the other man's name. She almost withdrew the question, except it seemed important, somehow, that she stand her ground. Why *did* he say so little to refute these aspersions when he must know of Mr Wickham's popularity amongst her neighbours, which made his account believable?

"Of what he has particularly accused me, I am ignorant."

Mr Darcy's words were stated flatly, with no hint of temper—or any other emotion, for that matter. Yet, had there been signs posted around his remark, they would all have declared 'Stop Speaking!' and 'Keep Away!' in angry red paint. With exclamation marks.

Of course, she knew she ought to drop the subject. It was stupid to provoke him, and none of her business besides. But an instant flare of frustration overruled good sense and polite conduct. She could very likely fall in love with him if she permitted herself, as unwise as that would be for a woman practically betrothed to another. Most probably, he would soon depart Netherfield, and she would not see him again. She would almost certainly never be alone with him again. Nothing in her life was her own, least of all him. But she would always wonder, and she refused to take the mystery into the rest of her life—not without a fight.

"He *says* you robbed him of a valuable living that was left to him in your father's will but in such language as enabled you to dismiss his claim. He *says* you, his boyhood companion, ruined his every prospect—coldly, cruelly, and deliberately."

"How can you be so certain he lies?" The question was spoken in the most arrogant, quelling of tones.

When she answered, her voice was quiet. "I was not, in the beginning. Your unkindness to me at the assembly in October made me ready to believe the worst of you."

His face twisted, and she turned back towards the flames. Before he could say anything else, she continued. "Closer observation of both you and Mr Wickham has enabled me to draw certain conclusions. You are a responsible gentleman who cares for his friends. You worry about the condition of the estate you helped Mr Bingley find. You likewise worry about him marrying my sister should she not truly love him. You worry about me wandering around out of doors in the cold. I cannot imagine the man I have come to know ignoring his father's final wishes. Neither has it escaped my notice that Mr Wickham told me, when still an utter stranger, all of his complaints, whilst you, who know me rather well by this point, remain silent regarding any of them. I suppose it is meant as judiciousness on your part, but I think you are wrong. *He* is neither silent nor troubled by discretion."

She heard his long sigh and did not know whether it was one of annoyance at her persistence or some other cause.

"He likely will not say overmuch while I remain in the area," he said after a pause. "He dares not risk a true confrontation."

He said nothing else for a long while, until Elizabeth decided it was all the answer he would give. She was startled when he again spoke.

"My father loved him like a son, and his father—the steward of Pemberley—like a brother." Elizabeth turned to look at him, but he only placed one booted foot onto the fender, leaning an elbow on one knee. "His father was an excellent man. I looked upon him almost as an uncle. He cared deeply for Pemberley, and taught me much regarding its management. He died in an accident within a six-month of my father. His son, however, was not cut from the same cloth."

Again, he lapsed into silence. There was something in his face, in his very posture, which radiated distress. It was as though he was hunched from a blow.

"I am sorry to have caused you the pain of reliving these experiences," she said at little more than a whisper. "Forgive me for having asked it of you."

He continued without acknowledging her apology. "In

his will, in addition to a bequest of one thousand pounds, my father asked that a valuable living be made available to Wickham, wishing for him to take orders. I knew he ought not to go into the church—imagine him, giving sermons on piety and goodness and then gambling away every penny he has! And gaming is the least of his sins. Not that he would ever fulfil the duties himself. He would hire a curate at starvation wages to perform all the actual labour of the parish, and use every penny it produced in riotous living. While he was beloved of his parents and mine, he is capable only of loving himself. Others do not exist for him the way they do for you and me. From a very young age, I suffered his vicious ways. I vowed I would not continue to do so."

"Did you not tell your father the truth about him?"

He shrugged. "When I was younger, yes, but Wickham was careful in his cruelty and clever in his victims. I do not possess his charm and charisma. It did not take me long to learn that if I were to do anything to interrupt the great friendship between him and my father, I would only look like a jealous prig, and eventually, someone or something I loved would be hurt. The only consequence he experienced for my openness was the delight of knowing I would endure yet another lecture or punishment for the sin of envy. After he poisoned my favourite dog, I learnt my lesson. I did not defy him again while my father lived."

She gasped, and he shook his head. "I apologise. You did not wish to hear a recitation of his sins, only an accounting of my refusal to give him the living."

"I would not blame you for declining to honour your father's bequest. He certainly should never be a clergyman."

"No, he should not, but refusing to give him the living was unnecessary. He did not want it. Within a month of his father's death, he told me he would not take orders and how insufficient a support the interest on his thousand pounds was—as though he had not already spent or lost it all! He said he meant to study law. I did not believe him, but I was perfectly willing to pay him to renounce all claim on the preferment. This he did, for the additional sum of three thousand."

"You paid him that much?" Elizabeth cried, shocked, reaching out, almost touching him before quickly drawing back.

"When the living became available a couple of years later, however, he expected me to give it to him."

"What? Why?"

"Because he wanted it. In his mind, it was his, and any money paid to him was simply what he deserved."

"It is unbelievable."

"Not to him. Naturally, I told him he had been compensated for the living and the matter was closed. I reminded him that however he influenced my father, he could not do the same with the son. I told him to never approach me again."

Mr Darcy held himself stiffly, not looking at her, his jaw as clenched as his fists, and appearing as though he wished to break something. Reflecting on what he had told her of Wickham's manipulations, she felt a sinking feeling in her stomach.

"Whom did he hurt?" she asked softly, her voice filled with sympathy.

Slowly, he turned to her, regrets a thousand fathoms deep in his dark eyes. "My sister."

Elizabeth bit her tongue against the shock and outrage she wished to express, knowing it would not help. Instead, she reached over and took his clenched fist in her hands.

"It happened last summer," he continued, his voice laden with sorrow. "There proved to have been a prior acquaintance between him and Mrs Younge, my sister's companion. Georgiana, whose affectionate heart retained a strong impression of Wickham's kindness to her as a child, was persuaded to believe herself in love and to consent to an elopement. She was then only fifteen, and easily influenced by the untrustworthy pair."

She squeezed his cold fist, a worthless gesture that could not begin to convey her horror. But he took a deep breath, and, to her great surprise, turned his hand in hers so that he was clasping it.

"You were able to prevent it?"

"I arrived unexpectedly a day or two before they planned to leave for Scotland. She could not bear the thought of disappointing me, and confessed all."

"Thank goodness." His skin was smooth, his grip a strong one; she had to force her eyes away from the sight of their joined hands.

"I have no doubt that Wickham is as bad as he ever

was. He will squeeze every shilling possible out of the men in his regiment. He cheats to win, and his note of hand is worthless when he loses."

His bitterness was understandable. Plainly, he had been taught from an early age—with horrific success—that to say a word against the man was to bring down hell upon those he loved.

"That is why you have not said anything in defence of your honour? You fear retribution."

He dropped her hand as though it stung him, and his voice was frosty. "Of course not. He is beneath my notice. My sister is now beyond his reach, and he can no longer injure me. Why should I care what a worm like him says?"

Elizabeth raised her brows. "Perhaps you should not. You might, however, care more about who he says it to." He could not want the entire neighbourhood believing the worst of him; his reputation must mean *something,* and she could not believe he despised them all enough to care nothing if anyone else was hurt.

His jaw clenched, and for a moment he looked so ferocious that she was tempted to shrink back. Just as quickly, his features froze into the impassivity she was accustomed to seeing in him.

She hated it.

Standing, he put another log on the fireplace, stirring up the embers and strengthening the flame. Elizabeth watched him perform the lowly task with competence, and sighed internally. She had no right, she knew, to judge a man who had been through such an awful struggle. It was easy to think his wealth and good looks protected him from misfortune. Plainly they did not.

"I think I shall write a book," she said, when the silence had grown wider than the physical separation between them. She hated that distance too. "I shall title it 'With Appreciation' and include long lists of things to be thankful for."

Her little ploy worked, for he turned and regarded her with a slight question in his eyes—obviously more than happy to turn the subject.

"I recall you declaring that such assistance is not useful."

"No, I said being *told* what I *ought* to find gratitude-worthy was of little benefit. My book will be the opposite. It will have, listed alphabetically, a thousand ideas of where to look for an ephemeral thankfulness when one is too overcome with melancholy to seek it out for oneself."

"Perhaps it is only in the search that one *can* find it. Perhaps, to the grieving man or woman, a thousand suggestions on the printed page would only be a thousand reproofs for not being able to like any of them."

"Well, plainly I shall not bring my book to *you* for publication, though you do write so well."

At her tease, he looked up at her sharply, the gap between them rapidly dwindling even though neither of them had moved.

"I believe I was complimented on volume and technique, rather than content." He smiled and the chamber shrank to a small and intimate place, a private world with room enough for only two.

Elizabeth caught her breath.

Mr Darcy was a handsome man; she had acknowledged that long ago. His looks—in conjunction with his wealth and bloodlines—made him a highly desirable personage. In his singular insult towards her at the assembly, he had declared himself unattainable to the populace. Probably, he did that at least once every time he went someplace new, before 'their young girls began dreaming dreams, and their older ones begat visions', of matrimony, of happily-ever-afters, quelling hopes before they could ever rise.

Heat flooded her face, and she quickly averted her gaze, struck by the realisation of what his insult in October had truly meant. He could not have made himself any clearer, from that first assembly: he was beyond their reach, all of them, but especially *her*. If the collective pride of Elizabeth, her family, and neighbours had been hurt by his words and he was disliked in return, he had cared not a whit.

It was an unkind fate, really, allowing her to see him as a man instead of an arrogant churl, and it was her own fault, for letting the insult no longer bother her.

Pushing her reflections aside, she said, "Perhaps I shall embroider each one on a pillow, then, and place them upon every surface of my sitting room. One will not be able to sit without shoving heaps of them out of the way. I must do something, you see, to keep them at the vanguard. I suppose my dreams of being a published author are in ruins, thanks to you, but you shall not prevent my career in needlework. If only I had thought to bring my workbasket. This place could use a few cushions."

He only smiled again at her—heavens, it was fortunate he had not tossed that smile about freely to the good people of Meryton, else he would have become the Pied Piper, with a long line of tittering girls following him wherever he went. She returned her gaze to the fire, contemplating the warmth of the room, the peace of her surroundings, and the company of a friend. It all combined to create a sense of serenity, a special kind of quiet she had not found in her own thoughts in days.

One moment she had leant her head against the arm of the banquette, only meaning to rest her tired eyes; the next she sat up with a start and looked about her in the confusion of the newly awakened. Mr Darcy was standing at one of the windows, looking out over the landscape. Thankfully, it still appeared to be daylight. She felt as though she had slept for hours.

"How long did I sleep? Do you know the time?" It would be all she needed, to be gone so long that her unobservant mother noticed and restricted even this little bit of freedom.

He turned away from the window. "Only an hour or so. I would have wakened you soon enough, but you appeared to need the rest."

She had seen the dark circles beneath her eyes in the looking glass that morning; obviously he had noticed them too. "My sleep has been...interrupted lately. I apologise for being poor company."

She stood, a little self-conscious, and crossed the room to don her coat, gloves, and hat.

"I am glad you were able to rest a little," he said composedly and began banking the fire in unspoken agreement that it was time to leave.

"Where does the staircase lead?" she asked, as though she were a dispassionate observer instead of an embarrassed one.

"There is a little landing and a door to the stone balconies. They are very small and only show a view of the surrounding forest." He opened the folly door, and the frigid air that flew inside was like a slap. Fortunately, the snow had stopped, and her coat was dry.

"I fear I did not pay close enough attention to my surroundings as we walked here, and I would not easily find my way home," she said. "If you could guide me to a more familiar part of the park, I would appreciate it."

"It would be my pleasure to escort you to the stile nearest Longbourn," he said, his tone formal.

And that was all. The distance between them widened again, to polite and formal. It was necessary, she knew, even vital that it be encouraged. But it felt like heart-break, even so.

Elizabeth tried to watch where they were going, but at one point she stumbled on a root, and he took her arm on the narrow path. Even at the place where the trail was smoother and widened enough to admit three easily, he did not let her go, although he said nothing.

It was odd, she thought, how synchronised was their gait; while she extended hers, he shortened his, as though they had practised it for ages.

"Oh, that path leads to Longbourn," she said. "I know where I am now."

He nodded, but did not withdraw his arm. "Did you find your 'one thing' to appreciate today?"

"Yes," she said immediately. "I am thankful for naps and the warmth of a fire on a cold day."

"That is two things," he pointed out.

"A very successful day, indeed," she replied. "Perhaps my father ought to take up walking rather than complaining of the flaws and foibles of his family and neighbours. It is of great benefit in reducing discontent."

"He *ought* to be able to acknowledge his gratitude from the comfort of Longbourn in the presence of five lovely and healthy daughters."

She looked up at him sharply, expecting mockery, but instead seeing only his earnest, steadfast gaze, and something in it made her blush.

"I am afraid my father would argue your point."

"You must give him a copy of your book, once it is completed."

She found her smile again and offered it freely. While smiling was not his habit, neither could she find much soberness in his easy regard. They did not speak until they reached the stile. Once again, without warning, he lifted her over it; this time she did not shriek.

When she was on the other side, he offered her a bow.

"I hope the rest of your day is a good one, Mr Darcy," she said. "Thank you, for everything."

He reached into a pocket and proffered an old-fashioned key over the fence; it was the one he had used earlier. "Feel free to make use of the folly as you wish. No one goes there. Truthfully, none of Netherfield's residents knows or cares where it is or has the inclination to discover it. You shall not be disturbed."

She took it from him. "Thank you again." The key was still warm from the heat of his body.

He nodded once, and it seemed like a dismissal. She faced Longbourn, not allowing herself to look back until she reached the path's turning. He stood there still, watching her. She lifted her hand in acknowledgement or farewell; he nodded brusquely, and began his walk to Netherfield.

I have discovered three things, she thought. *I am thankful for naps, for the warmth of a fire on a cold day, and for you, Mr Darcy.* Counting trees and sisters, she was up to five. That left only nine-hundred and ninety-five to go.

Seven

Elizabeth threw herself into the plans of her neighbours. She accepted every invitation to join parish committees, whether assembling Christmas baskets for the poor or sewing bandages for wounded soldiers. Even her father noticed, making a somewhat cynical remark regarding her sudden plethora of charitable projects. But he kept to their bargain and held his silence on the betrothal. Thankfully, she supposed he was leashing Mr Goulding as well, for at least there was no sign of him at Longbourn.

The truth was, she was talking—talking to everyone who would listen. And be she inside the walls of Longbourn, as she was now, or at the homes of her neighbours, Elizabeth was surrounded by avid listeners. She could not fix much that was wrong in her life, but she could certainly correct this one small thing—whether Mr Darcy ever learnt of it or not.

"He did what?" Charlotte asked, astonished. Charlotte had come to help her with the bandage sewing. It was her first opportunity since before the ball at Netherfield to talk privately with her friend.

"Mr Wickham poisoned Mr Darcy's favourite dog," she repeated. "All because he was jealous that old Mr Darcy loved his son. He is a viper."

It was vital that Charlotte be convinced of Mr Wickham's villainy. Elizabeth had saved the worst story she was willing to reveal for Charlotte—it went without saying that Miss Darcy's name and the story of her near ruin would never be mentioned. Sir William Lucas was the most notorious gossip in Hertfordshire. His eldest daughter, however, was as pious as she was practical, and while she was not inclined to indulge in the spreading of rumours, if she felt it was best for the greater community to know something, she would not hesitate to speak out.

"How did you learn of this?" Charlotte asked.

"Everyone at Netherfield knows, and naturally, Jane does too," Elizabeth fudged.

It was not a complete falsehood. Jane *did* know, because Elizabeth had told her. Being the unquestioning sort, her sister had not asked from where the information had come. However, Jane *might* have informed Mr Bingley of it, and thus the residents of Netherfield *might* all know the truth about Mr Wickham.

Jane and Mr Bingley's courtship was flourishing, as everyone in the area was aware. He appeared in Longbourn's front drawing room almost every day. At first, it *was* difficult for Elizabeth to broach the topic with Jane, to joyfully encourage her sister to speak of her feelings, but she was trying to be the person she *wished* she was— a girl less envious and bitter. As Jane confided in her, and as Elizabeth provided reassurance of Mr Bingley's devotion and advised her sister to make her feelings for him a bit more obvious, their sisterhood remained as healthy as Jane's romance. In an equation that did not quite make sense, the more goodwill and succour Elizabeth expended upon her sister, as well as on those other projects undertaken, the more she had for herself. At the very least, it left her with less energy to dwell upon her own sorrows.

Slumber and appetite remained elusive, however.

"This is terrible," Charlotte said.

Elizabeth agreed. "I could never have supposed a man so congenial could behave so wickedly. But then, we have always been warned of the danger of trusting in good looks alone."

"Perhaps he has since repented of his evildoing," Charlotte suggested. "He must have been just a boy."

Her sensible friend's belief in the man's possible reformation led Elizabeth to impart what several others in the community had already learnt; Mr Wickham was untrustworthy in the payment of debts. In Elizabeth's opinion, this was the news her neighbours—many of them being overfond of the card tables and small wagers —needed the most. Sir William Lucas was one of those who enjoyed the entertainment, much to his eldest daughter's disapproval.

Providentially, in this, Elizabeth was able to impart information that was from someone besides Mr Darcy. Her campaign to make known the truth of Mr Wickham's character had been taken up by others. "Mrs Lyford told me that her son Ernest—who is leaving for

Kintbury soon, as you know—demanded payment for a wager Mr Wickham lost last week, but Mr Wickham said he had no recollection of it! He made a joke of the whole thing and quite embarrassed Ernest. It was only a shilling or two, and he believed the man's word was good enough on such a small sum. Can you imagine Ernest Lyford inventing a false debt?"

"No, I cannot," Charlotte said, much alarmed.

"Mrs Lyford said that under ordinary circumstances, her son would have never mentioned it, but after hearing that Mr Wickham is not known for his honesty, he is warning his friends."

"Shocking!" Charlotte said. "The lieutenant must be naturally bad! I wonder whether Colonel Forster knows?"

"That, I have not heard. I hope someone of reputation and authority informs him." *Such as your father*, Elizabeth thought, but did not say.

"I suppose we ought not to believe anything Mr Wickham has said regarding Mr Darcy." Charlotte cast her a sly look. "By the way, I saw you go out on the terrace at the ball, *and* I saw Mr Darcy following you."

Elizabeth had long since prepared a response, should any one mention it. She rolled her eyes. "He was hardly following me. I did see him, as well as many others. It was so hot in the ballroom! Miss Bingley ought to have opened a few more windows! I suppose Mr Darcy also required a period in the cooler air. We spoke of inconsequential matters for a few minutes. I almost thought he might ask me for a set, but he did not. Did you see him dance with any lady beyond his own party?"

Elizabeth wanted to know who Mr Darcy had stood up with, but she had not dared ask her sisters for fear of betraying her growing feelings.

"He did not, as far as I know. I saw him later in the card room. I missed his return to the ballroom, as I did yours. I looked for you again and again, until finally, your mother told me you had returned home."

As much as Elizabeth did not like to lie to her friend, there was no choice. "I do not know what it was that evening, but I found the ballroom excessively hot. I then stayed out of doors for too long. It gave me the most dreadful headache, and I was forced to beg a ride home in one of Mr Bingley's carriages."

"Eliza! Did you wander off the terrace in the dark?"

"There were lamps," Elizabeth said, striving to sound sheepish. "They made the garden look so pretty. I did not go far, but too much of the icy air after so much heat quite ruined my evening."

Charlotte shook her head in disgust. "Your 'rambles' will be the death of you someday. When will you learn?"

"Come now, Charlotte, Mama's lectures were more than enough. Besides, there was no potential bridegroom in attendance, was there?"

This question set off Charlotte into her usual anxieties regarding potential spouses, and Elizabeth was content to let her go on regarding all who had attended and their relative suitability.

It had been a week of seeing neither hide nor hair of

Mr Darcy; the snow had prevented the Netherfield party's dining at Longbourn, and Mr Bingley arrived alone ever after. She walked out every day and always made the path to the folly her route. It was not as though she expected him to be there; he was scrupulously proper, and it would not have been right to turn their chance meetings into assignations. In fact, had he done so, she would have been forced to stop going out altogether; she had taken enough risk as it was. She would do nothing to jeopardise whatever brief interlude of freedom she had remaining.

Still, Elizabeth *missed* Mr Darcy. She missed talking to him and endlessly thought of their brief moments of contact—when he had held her hand or offered her his arm. Again and again, she pictured his smile, so rarely bestowed it became a treasure she would cherish for the rest of her life.

As though this newfound yearning was not bad enough, he managed to show he cared for her, even in his absence. The next time she went to the folly, she found a number of pillows, perhaps a subtle reminder of her little joke. A padded footstool and exceedingly comfortable chair appeared the following day, and the day after that, a chaise longue joined the rest—should she wish to nap again, she supposed. On Friday, there was a small table with a basket of cold refreshments perched upon it, and each day thereafter, it was refilled with fresh dainties and delicacies. Whenever she went, the folly fireplaces were burning warmly, and the wood piles replenished. She would not have been surprised had a maidservant and a cook materialised. It was almost as though she lived in a fairy tale, the way touches both large and small were continually added for her comfort and pleasure.

Elizabeth knew, as if he had left a note, that he was trying to give her something for which to be thankful, some little encouragements.

This morning, a new and popularly admired novel had been lying upon the table. She had opened it at once, hoping against all reason that she would find a message hidden in it. There was not. It would be inappropriate, considering they were not lovers. They were not even supposed to be friends, in the strictest sense. But he could leave a book there, convenient at hand should she care to read it.

"Eliza, I have repeated myself twice. Whatever is the matter with you?"

With a start, Elizabeth tore her thoughts away from Mr Darcy and her ever-increasing, hopeless feelings for him.

"I...I am so tired. I did not sleep well last night." It was another lie, and her eternal soul would be in danger if she continued along this path. "I apologise, Charlotte. What did you say?"

"I asked whether Mary will marry Mr Collins."

"She has not decided, she says."

"Will he return to Longbourn to gain his answer in person?"

"I do not know."

"He deserves to hear directly from her that she does

not want him, not through an impersonal letter!" Charlotte cried, her face flushing. "Forgive me, but Mary has raised his hopes, and if she will not have him, she ought to tell him so that someone else can take him!"

Elizabeth was so shocked at this outburst from her usually practical, stolid friend that she did not reiterate her own opinions of Mr Collins—after all, she had already shared them.

"I-I really cannot tell you what Mary intends to do. She will only say that she is considering it."

"It is most unkind of her to keep a good man on tenterhooks," Charlotte insisted. "It is not a difficult question. She must know whether or not she could tolerate him as a husband."

Elizabeth only stared at her friend for some moments. Charlotte's fists were clenched, and she leant forward as though she wished to choke explanations out of Elizabeth.

"My dear Charlotte, do you wish for his return for-for personal reasons?"

"Why not? If he is good enough for Mary, he is certainly good enough for me."

"I am surprised, that is all. You have agreed with me that he is not sensible."

Charlotte shrugged. "I do not ask for sense, only my own home, my own place in life as someone besides an impoverished relation. How much time do your parents spend with each other? My mother and father are hardly ever together. I suppose there are mealtimes, but not every one of those. Carriage rides, to church and the occasional village affair when our hems mustn't be spoiled. The infrequent rant, when he has done something stupid and must blame someone else for it. A few short hours a week in his company seems fair in exchange for an establishment of my own."

Elizabeth's brows rose. "Even..." She was too embarrassed to say what she meant, but Charlotte understood.

"The marital bed? I certainly could manage *him* in that, amongst other domestic arrangements. I would organise our lives according to my preferences, and once I had a child or two, that part of our union would be at an end."

Elizabeth could only shake her head. "If Mary decides against him, and he turns to you instead, I would be happy for you, of course." Despite her words, she was disappointed. *I knew she was practical, but this is taking it too far. At least Mr Goulding is not ridiculous.*

"If Mary refuses him, and he does not return to Meryton, his patroness will likely find him a bride who meets with her approval." Charlotte closed her eyes. Her cheeks were still stained pink. "*You* could never be happy with such a man as Mr Collins. No one who ever dreamt rosy dreams of a handsome prince could. But I never did. There is only one thing I have ever wanted, and that is a home that is not Lucas Lodge or any of my brothers'. I would be happy at Mr Collins's vicarage, and should he outlive your father, Longbourn will become his eventually. How you must hate me for saying that," she cried. "I would despise anyone who took *my* home away from *me*! I promise you, Eliza, that if you were to see that Mr Collins returns, even if—*especially* should Mary decide against him, I would ensure your mother, and any of your sisters who needed it would always have a home at Longbourn. A good home. A happy home. No stranger that he meets in Kent would do better for your family, I vow. I shall not bring this up again, but I had to say it once."

Eight

The following day, Elizabeth was about to make her escape to the folly. She was nearly breathless with the twin emotions of excitement and despair, expecting there would be a new gift or simple comfort, something from Mr Darcy demonstrating that he cared for her, that he wanted to *cheer* her. His *sole* purpose might be because he felt sorry for her, but that did not keep her from looking forward to his thoughtfulness, his...yes, *sweetness,* to say it another way.

But as she passed the parlour containing the pianoforte, there sat Mary at the instrument, quite alone, not touching it. There was something a bit discontented or annoyed in her pose. She was staring at the keys as if they had just bitten her, and she was considering biting them back. With a sigh, Elizabeth turned away from her escape to temporary freedom and entered the room.

"Is something the matter, Mary?"

Her sister turned slowly towards her, as though recalling herself from a great distance.

"The matter? No, nothing is wrong." A frown remained on her lips.

Elizabeth sat in a nearby chair. "Are you debating whether you should accept Mr Collins? I hope you do not consider it only to prevent us from losing Longbourn." Remembering Charlotte's passion for a home and not a man, she added, "However, there is nothing wrong with marrying to ensure your future security, if that is what you want most. Just be very certain you would be content with your choice."

Mary looked up and nodded slowly. "It is a very sensible reason for marriage. There is a solidity in his reflections which has often impressed me. He *might* be a very agreeable companion. Or, he might grow ever more ridiculous as he ages. It is difficult to say which."

"Very true," Elizabeth agreed, wondering how he could possibly become *more* ridiculous.

"Perhaps he would listen only to Lady Catherine de Bourgh. He certainly admires her greatly. If she is a sensible woman, I will admire her as well. But who can tell? I would not enjoy having another female instruct and direct me should I not respect her."

"That would be difficult," Elizabeth murmured.

"On the other hand, I feel well-suited to the life of a vicarage and to arranging my works for the benefit of a parish."

"You would make an excellent manager of any home, Sister."

"If it were only the parsonage, I would accept his offer. But there *is* Longbourn to consider."

Elizabeth did not know how to respond. Was not

eventually obtaining Longbourn, *retaining* Longbourn, the entire point?

"I cannot envision Mr Collins in Papa's role, can you?" Mary asked.

"Well, no. That is to say, not at this time."

"I cannot see it *ever*." Mary gazed up at the ceiling and sighed. "I believe I could help him in his calling as vicar. If I encouraged him to read and improve himself by such an example as mine, I might make something of him. However, acting as landlord and farming his acreage is another matter. I have no interest in agriculture or repairing roofs or raising barns and sheep. What am I to tell the tenants who require all the resources of proper management? That I shall pray for them?"

Elizabeth's brows raised. "You have a point." *An excellent one, as a matter of fact.* "If Jane marries Mr Bingley, I am sure he would advise you and Mr Collins."

Mary nodded seriously. "I have considered it, but he is only leasing Netherfield, and we have no guarantee he would remain close—or even that he is an excellent manager. I suppose his friend, Mr Darcy, might offer him instruction. Nevertheless, Mr Bingley has not yet proposed to Jane, and I wish to deal with facts only as they stand."

"That is also probably wise."

"To my understanding, our father spends very little time working on the estate, as far as attempts to increase yields and such. Still, he was born to his position and could likely do the barest minimum—that is, what he currently does—in his sleep. Our steward is a good one, but he is old. Can you imagine either of them writing out how to undertake their tasks so that I could learn them? Do you think they would recommend useful volumes for my study or allow me to trail them about to take notes?"

"No. I cannot see that," Elizabeth concurred.

"Nor do I really wish to learn. I do not *want* to be the last Bennet of Longbourn, Lizzy, known as the wife of the man who ran the estate into the ground. I cannot see Mr Collins doing any better at it than myself. He *might* be able to hire a competent steward, but he might just as easily hire someone awful. Obviously, I wish Papa to live to be a hundred, but I cannot count on that either, can I?"

"You are very wise, Mary, to take all these things into account. I only looked to the man himself, judged him harshly, and looked away."

She shrugged. "Your views are very different than mine. I do not expect a man to be congenial immediately. Most men require guidance and considerable effort, and it is my opinion that those who have less to offer in the way of looks and charm are more amenable to being trained up in the way that they should go."

Elizabeth was, to be truthful, quite astonished. Mary had depths she kept carefully hidden, or perhaps they were not always best displayed. Her younger sister tried very hard to perform well in all aspects of her life, and if she was a bit odd in her presentation, she should be encouraged in her efforts rather than mocked.

She even found herself wanting Mary's opinion on her own undesirable match.

"Do you suppose that if Mr Collins was not a young man, but an old one—Papa's age or more—do you suppose he could be similarly trained, even if one were not at all, um, attracted to him?"

Mary did not tease her to explain such a question, but approached it seriously, as she did everything. "It is possible, I suppose, especially if he were deeply entranced with his new wife. It would be difficult for her should she be repulsed by him. I do not mind Mr Collins's heaviness. I like a sturdy man, and I like his height. If he repelled me, I would probably have more reservations."

It was a fair answer, and a better one than Charlotte would have given.

"I wish you the best in your decision," Elizabeth said.

"I have some time," Mary replied, her frown easing. "Mr Collins promised to ask me at least two more times. He says it is good for a man to be crossed in love once or twice. I think Papa told him that, and he took it to heart."

Elizabeth hesitated, wondering whether she ought to say anything about Charlotte. In the end, she only did so because Mary should understand all the options open to her.

"Charlotte would like to marry Mr Collins, if you will not have him. She promises that if you refuse him, and she is successful at attaching him, she will ensure that any of us who need it will be always welcome and happy at Longbourn. Mama would be well-cared for, regardless of you marrying him."

Mary nodded contemplatively. "I am glad to know that. Charlotte would not have the same difficulties as I would, I think. She would be single-minded in devotion to her home and able to dismiss anything not directly related to it. I imagine her doing at least as well as Papa with the estate."

That is probably true, Elizabeth thought.

"I think you would do better in 'training up' Mr Collins, though," Elizabeth said, managing to find a smile. "Charlotte would likely ignore too much."

"Like the puppy who is not properly housetrained, he will continue to piddle on the floor if one does not make the effort to regularly take him on airings. I believe you are right," Mary agreed. "I only have to decide whether I want to make the effort."

"Mary is much wiser than I have given her credit for being," Elizabeth said to Mr Darcy. He was not at the folly, and her words sounded loud in the lonely room. Nevertheless, she told him the whole of the conversation as though he was sitting in the chair across from her.

Because I am going mad, she acknowledged, if only to herself.

Once again, she had arrived to find the fire roaring, built up for her by Mr Darcy—or at least, by his trusted servant. She lounged on the chaise and nibbled on a petite marchpane cake he had left. Her appetite was still absent, and she only picked at her meals, but she did not want him to think her unappreciative, thus she forced herself to consume something of each offering. The latest book he had left was a very good one, even though she could not pay attention long enough to devour it with her usual swiftness. Inevitably, she would come to a chapter's end and lose herself staring at the flames instead of continuing to read.

Today, she had wrapped herself in the folly's latest magical gift—a shawl spun of wool so fine and soft that it felt as though it was woven of clouds.

Sudden, overwhelming despair hit her, and tears burned her eyes. "How could you?" she cried. "Why do you spoil me like this, practically forcing me to fall in love with you?"

There was no answer, could be no answer. Mr Darcy was no fantastical beast, invisible to her, and she did not live in a fairy tale. He was a real person, who did many wonderful, considerate things for her so that she could more willingly, if still not happily, marry another man. He was kind, and yet the kinder he was, the more desolate she grew.

Roughly wiping away the wetness on her cheeks, she whispered to the flames, "I have a thousand entries for my book now. 'Tis your name, Mr Darcy, repeated a thousand times."

Nine

O nly a day later, Mr Bingley beamed across the dinner table at his affianced bride. The grand announcement had been made that very afternoon, and her mother and, more quietly, Jane, were in transports of joy.

Elizabeth was doing her best to keep a smile on her face. She was *very* glad for Jane; it was one less burden upon her heart to know that the happiness of one of her beloved sisters was assured. She could not help that the news also brought the knife edge of pain, and she did her best to suppress it, to fix only upon Jane's joy and thrust away her selfish sorrow.

It was nine days since Elizabeth had last seen Mr Darcy, and for the first time, she had not allowed herself to go to the folly that day. How could she continue to accept his gifts, even temporarily enjoying his borrowed largesse? It was wrong, and encouraging his well-meant intentions made her situation worse, not better.

Or so she repeated to herself in stern lectures, morning, afternoon, and night.

Unfortunately, she found that the ache of not having

even that slight connexion to him only intensified the pain of loving him.

It does not matter whether I go to the folly or not, she acknowledged. *The damage to my heart is already done.*

"Papa, I have a message I wish you to include in your next letter to Mr Collins," Mary said from her seat beside Elizabeth. "You must send him an invitation to return to Longbourn, as soon as possible, if you please. Much as I would like to invite him to join us for Christmas, because it is a particularly sociable time of year, a vicar must be with his flock during such an important season. Would you please ask him to return next Monday?"

Her father raised a brow. "I am to be forced to pen love letters now, am I? How low have I sunk, that I play matchmaker for Mr Collins?"

"I have not promised to marry him yet," Mary said. "You must not count upon that outcome."

"Oh, Mary, you have no compassion! You make a wreck of my poor nerves!" Mrs Bennet cried, even though she was too delighted with Mr Bingley and Jane's engagement to truly put much energy into her complaint.

Elizabeth covered Mary's hand with her own. "You have made a decision?" she whispered.

"I am *mostly* decided," Mary murmured. "I shall know for certain when I see him, I feel sure. Thank you for speaking with me in a rational manner yesterday. It was very helpful."

"Any time, my dear sister."

Mary leant over a bit closer, ensuring they would not be overheard. "Should you ever need to discuss any concerns of your own, please know that I possess a willing ear."

Elizabeth turned sharply towards her, but Lydia chose that moment to make a loud announcement.

"Lieutenant Wickham has deserted his regiment! Penelope Harrington told me that Mr Harrington confirmed it with Colonel Forster. Wickham struck the quids, all the fellows say. To Mr Denny alone, he owes a mint."

"Watch your language, Lydia!" Mr Bennet warned severely. "No one at the dinner table wishes to hear about the gambling obligations of *anyone*. The topic is closed."

Lydia rolled her eyes. "They say he owes even more to the merchants in town!"

"Lydia!" her father reprimanded.

"I am not speaking of *gambling* but of *debt*!" Lydia insisted. Kitty giggled. Mr Bennet returned to his meal.

As Jane blushed and Mrs Bennet began another soliloquy upon her nerves, Elizabeth struggled to contain her temper. Her father overlooked his own flaws as easily as he ignored the comportment of his family.

Mr Bingley chimed in as though there was no impropriety in the manners of her younger sisters. "Actually— and just between ourselves—Darcy has stated his intention of making the merchants of Meryton whole. I believe everyone in town knows his history with the despicable Wickham, but Darcy says he ought to have warned people about his old friend sooner. I think he takes too much upon himself. I, personally, heard enough to know that much of Wickham's treachery was fairly public, and any person foolish enough to take his note likely deserved what he got. But Darcy will not hear of anyone in the area being hurt." He shook his head in a mixture of admiration and wonder.

"Where *is* your friend, Mr Bingley?" asked Mrs Bennet. "We have not seen him at Longbourn in days. I hope he is not feeling poorly."

It was an obvious bid for gossip, and it was Elizabeth's turn to blush—for more reasons than her mother's ill manners.

Mr Bingley showed no sign of reproach; he only continued in affectionate commentary. "Darcy is always so busy, with so many duties and tenants, not to mention his devotion to the needs of his entire family, especially his young sister. He needed a rest, and Netherfield has proved the perfect place for him to find it. He mostly spends his days riding out, although he has gone to London twice—only for the day, though."

Elizabeth listened with rapt attention.

"He is not a very sociable fellow, that Darcy," said Mr Bennet. "'Tis one of the things I like best about him."

"He is a fine man," Mr Bingley declared, smiling widely at Jane. "It would be impossible to ask for a superior friend. When I informed him I meant to ask for Miss Bennet's hand today, he said I would be a fool if I did not, and that I could not have made a better choice of bride."

Jane returned his smile until Kitty's coughing fit brought forth another lecture from Mrs Bennet regarding her nerves. Talk returned to wedding plans and shopping campaigns, and while fruit tortes, apple cake, and even sugar plums were served, Elizabeth made an effort to eat. It all tasted like dust in her mouth.

She had not needed to go to the folly to see Mr Darcy's latest kindness; hiding from it, and him, had failed utterly. His goodness had come to her in her own home.

Mary was entertaining them all with a tune on the pianoforte when Mr Bennet tapped on Elizabeth's shoulder.

"Come to the book-room, please," he murmured.

The blood in Elizabeth's veins froze in a sudden panic. She imagined fleeing from the room and running for the remainder of her life.

Her father had timed his request perfectly. Elizabeth would not disrupt the evening by showing her defiance. How could she bring darkness to her family while they celebrated Jane's engagement? She paused to appreciate the way Mr Bingley sat watching his future bride with every sign of contentment. Knowing how overjoyed Jane was, and what a good man he was, gave Elizabeth the strength to endure whatever her father had to impart.

She followed him to his book-room, feeling as though

she were headed to the guillotine, despite her resolve. She sat, staring at a point beyond his head.

"Well, Lizzy," he said, after a few moments of uncomfortable silence, "you have done yourself no favours these last two weeks."

She brought her gaze to his face, wondering if he somehow knew *everything* she had been doing. Had he followed her to the folly? Never mind that she and Mr Darcy had not been there together except that first time; obviously it was not de rigueur to spend all of one's time in a folly furnished like a fairy tale cottage, enjoying the comforts placed there by a gentleman few knew she considered a friend.

Her father was not looking at her, but at the ceiling. His fingers were steepled in front of his face—which, contrary to her expectations, showed no signs of anger.

"I do not understand what you mean, Papa."

His eyes met hers. "You have been wandering about in the out of doors for hours, flitting around to every parish committee as though you fear for your eternal soul, then moping about the house with a hang-dog expression, even refusing to eat. Your mother believes you are coming down with some ailment and wishes to call in Mr Jones."

His complaints were so patently unfair, that for a moment she was tongue-tied. "You cannot expect me to be overjoyed that I am to be married off to a man old enough to be my grandfather?"

"*That* is a dramatic exaggeration, as you well know," he said with a condescending smile she despised.

"Plainly, giving you time to accustom yourself to the marriage is doing you no good. You asked for a period of reflection, and I agreed, but you have used it to embrace self-pity. You cannot recognise your own best interests. We shall be dining with the Gouldings Friday evening. Your betrothal will be announced to the family then."

"Friday?" she cried in shock and disbelief. "But it is already Thursday! Surely you could find enough compassion in your soul to wait until after Jane is wed."

"Your mother plans a prodigiously excessive celebration to accompany Jane's nuptials. You would not want that, and it would be inappropriate given Goulding's recent bereavement. He and I are agreed it is best for you to wed quietly and to do it soon."

"I hate you." She believed it, too, with every piece of her person.

He closed his eyes briefly, and his voice was rougher than it had been a moment ago. "I would rather have your hatred, knowing you will be well provided for all the days of your life, than retain your affection knowing it is accompanied by an uncertain future."

"Spare me whatever stories you tell yourself so that you can sleep at night," she hissed. "You are not insisting on this for my sake or that of my mother and sisters. Jane will soon be well-married. I shall always have a home with her. You know as well as I do that Mr Bingley is an excellent man. He will ensure my mother and sisters have everything they require. Mary might accept Mr Collins, and Mama would not even have to leave Longbourn. This has *nothing* to do with what is best for me and everything to do with your irresponsible, selfish behaviour. What possessed you to put yourself into so much debt? You are no better than Mr Wickham!"

His expression turned to granite. "You believe you will never wish for a home of your own, that you would not enjoy being mistress of your own future? You do not know yourself. The vicar has already been informed. The first banns will be called this Sunday. We will not discuss this further. Go." He pointed at the door.

His mind was made up, and she would have no further reprieve. Without another word, she stalked from the room.

Ten

Elizabeth lay awake all night long, staring at a shrinking candle until it sputtered out. At first light, she dressed in her warmest clothing and quietly left the house before her father was likely to have left his rooms. She was determined to arrive at the folly early and send a message with the servant who lit the fires that she needed, desperately and at all costs, to speak to Mr Darcy.

I am going to run away. I shall take a position as a governess or a-a bootblack. Mr Darcy will agree to give me a reference. Papa cannot threaten Jane with unwanted matrimony now that she has accepted Mr Bingley's suit. My life shall be my own, however lowly.

One phrase rang as a drumbeat in her head: *I cannot, I cannot, I will not!*

However, when she reached the folly at last, no fires burned. "No!" she screamed aloud to the empty room, throwing herself to the hearth rug before its barren, cold grate. "No! You cannot leave me alone now, when I need you most!" The sobs she had been unable to free in the night tore from her, and she simply let them come, crying until she was spent and sore.

The morning's panic diminished with her tears.

I ought to have expected this, she thought. *I have never been here this early.* Picking herself up off the floor, she flung off her hat, wrapped herself in the woollen shawl, huddled onto the chaise, and stared at the bleak hearths.

She was so weary of fighting despair, of trying to make sense of her life. How was she to ever feel peaceful again? Could she really subject Jane and even Mary to embarrassment, to place them in the awkward position of trying to explain a runaway sister at such a vulnerable time? If she outright refused the match, could she truly subject her family to ruin? Was Mr Goulding cruel enough to enforce his threats? For the first time, she considered the desperation that must have fuelled his dark promise. She had known him all her life; he had never been anything except kindly. Would there be any chance, before the betrothal announcement, to simply speak to him and ask him for reprieve? If he would not, could she summon the courage to do what was required?

The questions went round and round in her brain. Having eaten so little over the last two weeks and slept not at all in two days, that despite the frigid temperature, she fell fast asleep without answering any of them.

When Elizabeth awoke, it was full light. Both fire-places were burning, but the flames were weak. That she had slept through someone entering and lighting both fires only showed how exhausted she had been. Muzzyheaded, she struggled to one side of the room and then the other, adding wood to keep the fires alive, something she had grown rather adept at doing. She scrubbed her face with her hands, taking several deep breaths, trying to calm herself.

Had Mr Darcy been here himself while she slept? Had he watched over her for a time?

Do not be fanciful, she warned herself. *He has always had the greatest respect for me and regard for my privacy.* Yet despite that, she had the feeling that no servant had been here.

That was when she noticed the covered dishes.

There was an entire cold collation, crumpets and sliced roasted beef, ham, several different cheeses, short-bread, and some type of meat pasties—enough to feed ten distressed females.

A single tear slid down her cheek. This time he had left not simply a few treats, but an entire, hearty meal, as though he knew she desperately needed one.

Mr Darcy had come and gone; she was certain of it. It did not matter that she had not seen him, for as soon as she had awakened, reason returned, and Elizabeth knew he would never provide her with a reference to take on the work of a menial. How could she become a governess? *She* had never even *had* a governess. She and her sisters had only learnt and studied as had suited their whims. While Elizabeth considered herself as intelligent as the next person, there were notable gaps in her educa-tion. No truly good home would choose *her* to educate their precious children. Staring at her hands, she compared their condition to the competent, work-rough-ened ones of Mrs Hill. Her own soft skin testified to its ignorance of heavy labour.

I am not lazy, but neither am I stupid. I was raised as a lady and taught to manage a home, plan menus, super-vise the needs of a large household, stitch, make polite conversation, and ensure my guests are welcomed and well fed.

"I can organise a village fête, but I can hardly organise a new station in life!"

To make such an enormous change would require assistance. The only person she could think to ask was her uncle, and she had not yet been successful in getting a letter to him. The first banns would be called before she could reach him, and it would put him in the awful position of defying her father. He might, possibly, do it, even though it would cause a rift, but, as Papa had pointed out, she would only be placing the burden of her care upon his shoulders. Mr Gardiner would never agree to help her find employment.

It was a temptation to stay hidden in the folly for as long as she could get away with it, but when all was said and done, she already had her answers. She would not allow her entire family to be ruined when it was within her power to prevent it. The markers had been called in. She was either brave enough to face the situation forth-rightly or not the woman she had always thought herself.

Mr Goulding was not ridiculous; he was a kindly man she had always cared for and looked upon as a near relation, despite the actual distance in the blood connexion. He had been a widower for ten years and now had lost his only son, casting him into a desperate state of grief. Her father was in no position to negotiate with him. If she asked very carefully and with great sympathy, perhaps Mr Goulding might agree to wait a suitable mourning period. Elizabeth could say it was to keep up appearances on his end, and so the neighbourhood would not believe her a fortune hunter. Still, at his age, once the circumstances of the entail were known, it was unlikely that anyone would truly blame him for taking a wife so much his junior, or even think poorly of her for marrying him, since she had so little.

She felt weak, and her head ached. Slowly, methodically, she forced herself to eat some of the food Mr Darcy had provided. She would need her strength for what was to come.

Only after she had eaten did she notice the carved wooden writing desk. Beside it was perched a perfect yellow rose in a crystal bud vase.

The desk was a beautiful thing; she set it upon her lap and opened the compartments. She found everything needed for letter writing and several bound notebooks.

Setting it aside, Elizabeth wandered to the window. If it had snowed, she could not tell. Drops of water dripped off the leaves, and the sky was a murky grey gloom, but it was not raining. Somewhere, above those dark clouds, the sun shone—invisible at the moment, but there, nevertheless.

The morning passed slowly, and yet, too quickly.

She knew her family might already be looking for her at home before she removed writing supplies from the pretty little lap desk, and began her letter.

Dear Mr Darcy,

I should have thanked you before this for the many little comforts you have provided during these last two weeks, but in truth, my head has been too bewildered, and even now, I cannot answer for the coherence of my thoughts. I have also known that I should put a stop to your generosity and any letter I write to you must be one which makes it clear that I can no longer accept your generosity, even though it is of a temporary—and enchanting—nature. I ought to have done it sooner, but I could not quite bear to. Nevertheless, I must do so now.

Before I continue this missive, I beg leave to relate how I spent the morning. First, I partook of the delicious meal you provided—I must say, the shortbread was the best I have eaten. I then sat in the warmth of gentle flames in the most comfortable chair ever constructed, propping my feet upon a perfectly sized footstool, and finished the novel thoughtfully left for my entertainment. Self-Control had a most pleasing conclusion, especially after all the convolutions poor Miss Montreville endured; however, I do wonder at her father's dying of grief merely upon contemplation of his daughter's vacillating defiance. My papa would not have lasted into his fourth decade, had filial obedience been a necessary element of longevity. I suppose the Bennets of Longbourn are resilient, if nothing else.

Oh, I nearly omitted an important correction. I climbed the stairs to the stone balconies you informed me held views of nothing and nowhere. You were mistaken. The vista is of ancient oaks guarding it from the sight of any who do not pay the price of finding it. Perhaps it is not a scene framed in classical beauty— both Longbourn and Netherfield are quite hidden—but in what I could not see, I could imagine a different view, perhaps even a different future than the one I have been dreading. If I cannot see it, that means it has not yet happened. Happiness might be hidden, and yet be on the horizon.

I spent this leisurely morning of reading wrapped in the loveliest, softest shawl in the world, and pretended— just this once, I promise—that it was your embrace keeping me warm and secure.

My father has informed me that my period of grace, such as it was, is at an end. I go with my family this evening to dinner at the home of my soon-to-be betrothed. The announcement will be made then, and the banns called beginning Sunday. The next time we meet—which I suppose may be at Jane's wedding, for Mr Bingley mentioned you had agreed to stand up with him—I shall be known as Mrs Goulding.

I just want to say—the last two weeks have been the most caring and considerate I have ever experienced. I shall keep the rose and press it to remind me, during *whatever comes, of my sincerest appreciation for all you have done. My book is filled and finished now.*

I will only add, God bless you.
    Elizabeth Bennet

She sanded and sealed the letter, placed it atop the writing desk, and set that upon the footstool where it would be obvious. Painstakingly, she packed away the crockery in the basket, folded the shawl, and banked the fires. Gently, she set the key to the folly on top of the letter.

At the doorway, she took one last look around the cosy little room, engraving the scene upon her memory. She glanced at the perfect rose clutched in her gloved hand. Then, she shut the door firmly, hearing the soft click of the latch, and walked away without looking back.

Eleven

Elizabeth thought about wearing her mourning crape to this meal, to make it obvious to everyone her opinions on this betrothal. But she knew she must be very careful. She might not, probably *would* not be able to avoid matrimony, and Mr Goulding would then rule over her existence. If she was to somehow establish a happy life for herself, she must avoid offending him.

It was patently unfair.

Yet, she remembered the promises she had made to herself as she looked out over the folly's balcony. Her father had ordered her to grow up, to cut her childish dreams like leading strings.

Well, she was trying, endeavouring to move past the severed sting of loss, towards the happiness hiding just beyond the clouds. She *would* find it.

The Bennet women travelled as a cramped group to Haye-Park, squeezed together in the carriage while Mr Bennet rode on the box with their old driver. Elizabeth wore a demure gown in forest green, a dark shadow beside her sisters, dressed in paler shades.

To all outward appearances, she remained unaffected. She smiled at Lydia's joke, lent Kitty a handkerchief, asked Mary what time she expected Mr Collins on Monday, and mediated a dispute between Kitty and Lydia regarding who was taking up the most room on the seat. Or perhaps she was not quite so skilled at hiding her inner turmoil as she believed, for Jane, on her left, asked Elizabeth whether she was feeling well with true worry in her voice, and Mama, on her right, fretted aloud that she had stayed out of doors too much in the cold weather and joined too many parish committees for her health.

Their concern meant something, even if it could not heal her. She would always have her family's support, she knew; it reinforced her determination to do what she could to prevent their ruin. Once she heard the news, Jane would mourn with her, and would help her to adapt and adjust to her new role with delicacy and kindness. Elizabeth would have a lovely home, and her temporal needs met. It would not be horrible. She would make certain of it.

"I do not understand why Mr Goulding is entertaining so soon after Reginald's death," Mrs Bennet declared with a disapproving sniff.

"Mama, you know what Papa said about Mr Goulding's loneliness. It is only dinner, and we are related, albeit distantly. Poor Mrs Goulding. I wish I had some way of comforting her," Jane said.

"She and her husband were always bickering." Lydia

shrugged. "I do not think I ever saw them together but that they were at loggerheads."

"Just because they did not always get along does not mean that she is not concerned for her husband's immortal soul," Mary pontificated. "Young Mr Goulding was known for his drunken displays. I would be terrified for him, were I her."

Elizabeth sighed.

In the distance, the lights of Haye-Park shone from every window in an impressive display. Once having been an Augustinian priory, it was a stately example of Elizabethan architecture set upon a thousand acres of parkland.

Of this place, I shall have to be mistress. Of its rooms, I must become familiarly acquainted. It was a grand and glorious mansion, but to be the mistress of Haye-Park's one hundred and thirty rooms only added to the dread in her heart. *Courage, Elizabeth! You will rise to any challenge!*

A liveried footman let down the steps and opened the door, helping each lady from the vehicle. With Mr Bennet, they walked up together to the marbled front entrance.

Elizabeth had entered Haye-Park at least two dozen times without ever feeling a real admiration for it. It was too large and cold; even when the fireplaces were lit and candles brightened the spaces, it seemed every window was winking at her in frigid disdain. In the portraiture lining the walls of ancestors long since buried, she imagined a universal look of dissatisfaction.

I do not want to be here either, she thought at them. *I shall do my best to improve the surroundings for all of us.*

On reaching the spacious lobby above, they were shown into a very pretty drawing room, lately fitted up with greater elegance and lightness than the apartments below. It was in this chamber that their host greeted them.

Elizabeth held herself stiffly, with what she hoped was a poised and pleasant expression, although it seemed that everyone must recognise it for false. Thankfully, after a brief minute of courteous acknowledgement that included her sisters and herself, Mr Goulding greeted her parents. Young Mrs Goulding appeared pale and delicate in her black gown, her manners perfectly polite, as though their presence in a house of mourning was an ordinary event. Did she know why the Bennets were here, intruding upon her grief?

It was in that moment that she saw the room held another guest—Mr Darcy.

Elizabeth was unprepared, embarrassed, her cheeks overspread with the deepest blush, only barely preventing a gasp of astonishment. How could she keep up her bid for courage, endure this entire performance while *he* watched? He gazed at her with an intense look that evidently meant *something*, although she could not fathom what.

"I believe you are all acquainted with Mr Darcy," Mr Goulding said genially. They each nodded, and her father raised a brow. Plainly, he had not expected this addition to their party either.

During dinner, and to her credit, Mrs Bennet tried to keep the conversation going, but her enquiries about his latest favourite potion or poultice, which usually Mr Goulding was pleased to share, fell rather flat.

Elizabeth could not help taking sidelong glances at Mr Darcy. Was her longing for him, although determinedly hidden, as obvious to all as had been her earlier disquiet? He was even more handsome than her memories had preserved, but at least his presence by her side gave her motivation to keep her dignity intact, no matter how awful it would be to suffer through this evening. Liveried footmen served her sisters portions of roast and lamb, but Mr Darcy expertly attended to Jane's plate and her own. He said nothing to her beyond a few commonplaces, but his steady, earnest gaze was nearly as comforting as though he had taken her hand.

Was that why he had come? As a support and comfort? She was being fanciful again, no doubt, but how had he garnered an invitation to a private family meal?

Beneath Mr Goulding's gracious manners, one could tell that he was distracted. Given the death of his only son a few weeks ago, it was understandable. Her own father, when not applying himself to his food, watched Mr Darcy. As the meal progressed, Elizabeth found it all quite odd.

At long last, Mrs Goulding suggested the ladies excuse themselves, and they made their way back to the drawing room where they had first congregated. If Elizabeth had hoped Mrs Goulding would provide any clues to the reason for Mr Darcy's presence, she was to be disappointed. The lady asked whether any of them played, and Mary quickly volunteered. They found seats while she thumbed through the music at the brightly polished pianoforte. The housekeeper brought tea and biscuits.

The proceeding interval felt like the longest of Elizabeth's life. Mary played several pieces while the clock ticked on and on. Lydia fidgeted. Kitty coughed. Mrs Bennet began a dispute with Lydia on the elegance of a new style of sleeves, which Jane attempted to arbitrate. Idly, Elizabeth wondered why the best moments raced by at breakneck speed, while the worst ones dragged— each second seeming to last an hour. And yet, every minute spent here was a minute she was not betrothed. She struggled between wanting this interlude to last forever and wishing to get it over with. She dared not even hope that Mr Darcy was arguing her point. What influence had he on her father or Mr Goulding? Finally, the door opened. Elizabeth turned to it, the blood pounding in her temples—*the moment* had arrived.

But it was not the gentlemen. It was the housekeeper.

She strode directly to Elizabeth. "Excuse me, miss, but you are wanted," she murmured.

"Lizzy? Why would they want you? Lizzy?"

Elizabeth ignored her mother's queries and followed the servant.

Ice travelled through Elizabeth's limbs and up through her facial nerves, leaving her feeling frozen inside. She could walk, she could converse, but she had already begun quelling all the pieces of self that *made* her herself, crushing them down and flattening them so they would fit into the small space henceforth to be allowed. She squared her jaw. *Mr Goulding is a decent, sensible man*, she reminded herself. *I will be good to him, and he will return that respect. I will build a life worth living.*

The housekeeper opened a door; she went through it, hearing the soft click as it shut behind her.

Elizabeth found herself in a spacious library she had never seen before. Mr Goulding and her father stood as she entered. A surreptitious glance around the room confirmed that Mr Darcy was nowhere to be seen.

"Please, Elizabeth, be seated," her father said.

Spine straight and chin lifted, she obeyed.

The gentlemen seated themselves across from her. Mr Goulding did not seem to know where to look, but her father eyed her sternly.

"A few weeks ago, I informed you that I had agreed to a marriage between you and Mr Goulding. In the interim, circumstances have somewhat altered. Mr Goulding would still like to offer for you. However, you are not to take into consideration any debts between myself and him. The choice to agree to his proposal or reject it is entirely your own. My opinion remains the same. It would be an excellent match, and you could not acquire a finer husband." Mr Bennet's expression softened. "I hope you understand, Lizzy. I would not have parted with you to an unworthy man."

With those words, he quit the room.

Reeling from her father's pronouncements, Elizabeth stared at Mr Goulding, who still avoided her gaze; his embarrassment was obvious.

"I say," he began. A long pause followed. "I say," he tried again. He scratched his head, shook it, and smiled ruefully. "Difficult to know the right words. I shall begin with an apology. I assure you, I did not mean to cause you distress. Your father thought, after your initial, um, surprise, upon due consideration...well." He cleared his throat. "I always thought you a sensible, intelligent girl. I wished my son had looked your way, even suggested it once. I have always known you would make an excellent mistress for Haye-Park, for my tenants. Even had no sons been born of the marriage, I would not have been sorry." He flushed. "I am getting ahead of myself—or do I mean behind? It has been a long while since my salad days. I suppose what I am saying is that my offer is open to you, should you ever wish to receive it. I know my age, and I understand if you wish to wait and see whether a younger fellow turns up."

There was another long pause until Elizabeth found her tongue at last.

"Please, sir, accept my thanks for the compliment you are paying me. I am very sensible of the honour of your proposal, but I am, perhaps, not so sensible as you believe. It is impossible for me to do otherwise than think of you as a respected family relation, almost an uncle, and I am afraid I must decline solely for that reason. Your age does not enter into it."

She offered him a small smile, one both sincere and apologetic, acknowledging to herself for the first time the flattery of his offer. He rose; she stood with him.

He held out his hand. "No hard feelings, what?"

She shook it firmly. "Of course not, sir. You are very kind."

Bowing, he escorted her from the room.

Elizabeth could not believe she was free of the betrothal. She could not believe it during their farewells to the Gouldings. She could not believe it during the long carriage ride home, while her mother interrogated her regarding the whys and wherefores of her thankfully brief separation from their party; not even knowing *what* to answer, she referred all questions to her father, much to Mama's dissatisfaction.

Arrived at Longbourn again, she could only grin when Mama prevented Papa's escape into his book-room with her demand for explanations—and when he looked to *her* as if *she* might rescue him, she grabbed Jane's hand.

"Jane, what dishes have been planned for your wedding breakfast? I cannot believe we have not yet spoken of menus!"

Jane, whose own concern—albeit much more quietly demonstrated—had been rather obvious, gave her a relieved smile. Chattering away about meal courses and clothing, they ascended the stairs together. They spent a happy hour in her chamber discussing all things to do with the wedding before Elizabeth finally found herself alone.

She stretched out upon her bed, staring at the ceiling, trying to examine her feelings as they swelled within her. There was relief, certainly, and joy that her freedom had been restored. Intrigue, as well, at Mr Darcy's role in it all. But there were too many sensations to name, overwhelming every attempt to categorise or deal with them. She laughed quietly to herself.

It was all simply...unbelievable.

Twelve

Elizabeth roused the next morning with the sunrise. Dressing warmly, she slipped out of the house with only one direction in mind—the path to the folly.

No one shall be there. It will be locked, empty and cold, she told herself to temper her hopes of finding Mr Darcy there. Despite telling herself it was a ridiculous waste of time to go so far, especially since the recent snow made the path difficult, it seemed her feet had made a decision of their own accord, and there was but a single direction they were willing to walk.

What does it matter? I shall go to the folly, and then go home. Nevertheless, it was all she could do to stop herself from breaking into a run on the slippery surfaces. *Would* he be there? How she longed for it to be so!

She felt her heart beating hard as she approached the cheerful green door. Reminding herself it would be locked, and that she absolutely *did not* expect anyone else to be there at such an early hour, she touched the handle.

The door opened easily, the warmth from the interior rapidly heating her skin. Or perhaps it was her own blush, because there in front of the fireplace stood Mr Darcy.

He turned when she entered, and Elizabeth found herself more tongue-tied than she had ever been. To cover her sudden confusion, she pulled off her gloves and set them on the table holding the writing desk, then removed her coat and hat, hanging them on the hooks near the door. Realising that the letter she had written to him was gone, she suddenly wished she had not been so free with her pen. Why had she done it? He could not possibly return her feelings; they were too strong, having grown far beyond compassion and those of a friend. Embarrassment burned through her.

Without volition, her feet carried her to the hearth. Even when she stood beside him, Elizabeth could not think what to say. In the letter, she had admitted that she wanted his arms about her. She had depended upon on it being a few months, at least until Jane's wedding, before she had to face him again, and by then, she would be married to someone else. Both of them would have forgotten, or at least ignored, their temporary friendship; there would have been little need to apologise for an honesty for which he might never have wished.

His expression was flat, and he showed no sign of pleasure at seeing her. Any hopes she had harboured, and her heart with them, sank.

"I owe you my deepest apologies, Miss Elizabeth," he said, his manner stiff and formal.

"Do you mean for being here? You could not know I

would return."

"As a matter of fact, I was fairly certain you would come this morning. You are owed explanations."

"I only need one. Why were you at Haye-Park last evening?"

He sighed. "If you would like to sit, I have a rather lengthy story to offer."

She nodded and crossed to the chair; he pulled the banquette closer to her, seating himself on it.

Scrubbing his face with both hands, he took his time making a beginning. "I suppose I should start by telling you how I have wished I could retract my words, spoken so hastily at that assembly. Never has a man spoken so foolishly. Hardly a week passed from that moment before I thought you the handsomest woman of my acquaintance."

She looked up at him sharply. "I-I did not realise..."

His expression was wry. "My conscience was still reasonably clear, however. I had no intentions, and although I was attracted to you, my long habit of selfishness withstood any correction to my manners. It was not, in fact, until the night of the ball at Netherfield that I experienced the beginnings of true remorse. I had been determined to indulge my fancy for you by claiming a set, and when I spotted you escaping the ballroom shortly after appearing—for I was watching for your arrival every minute—I followed you out of doors immediately. You know what I then learnt. I told myself it did not matter for my sake. I had not considered you in any way eligible. Yet I felt the most bitter recriminations towards your father and fate, a terrible fury that you were subjected to this distress, that such beauty and wit would go to some undeserving ancient wretch who could never appreciate his good fortune."

Elizabeth raised her brow, unsure whether insult or flattery was uppermost in his revelations. "Um. Thank you?"

He sighed. "I usually ride most mornings. Instead of doing so, the day after the ball I began walking a path I had noticed you on once before, one leading between Longbourn and Netherfield, although I had not acknowledged to myself that I was searching for you. My unreasonable happiness when I discovered you upon it on the second day was clue enough to dispel any excuses I might have entertained. For the first time, I admitted my great danger. By the end of that first walk, most of my pretensions were in tatters. I conceded that while the inferiority of your connexions was a hindrance to any intentions I might have harboured, they could not be to Bingley. In fact, I was envious that his station in life was such that he might pursue a match which I could not."

"Fortunately for you, I was at that time practically engaged to another," she said archly, regretting more than ever her honest admissions in that letter. "I would by no means upend any favoured opinion of yours."

Mr Darcy sighed again, and did something startling —he reached over and brushed her cheek, a featherlight touch that she nevertheless felt in every part of her body. His eyes caught and held hers; she was the first to look away.

"The next day, I actively searched for you. I was beginning not to care for any of my former sentiments—the thought of you wandering the park, alone in your grief, was untenable. By the time we parted, it was all I could do not to declare my own love for you. I do not think I slept a wink that night."

She opened her mouth to say something, but shock at his admission—and in disbelief that she had heard correctly—made it impossible to form words. Before she recovered her senses, he continued his explanations.

"I knew I had to stop meeting you, but I felt compelled to ensure you had a place of refuge and relief. I had come upon this folly once before, and the idea came to me to procure its key and stock a supply of fire-wood. When I brought you within, I was afraid that I would succumb to the danger of your appeal if I did not leave immediately. I was right," he said in a low voice. "I think I might have resisted for at least another day, had you not fallen asleep on this wretched banquette. Watching over you while you slept, realising it was the first and last time I would ever have that privilege... the thought was abhorrent."

It was her turn to reach over; she took his larger hand in hers, marvelling at the differences between them. The entire experience had become incredible; he could not possibly be confessing feelings as strong as her own. His hand became the only certainty in the room as he covered hers, squeezing it. Abruptly, with something like agony in his expression, he broke the connexion and practically leapt to his feet, going to the hearth and gripping the mantel.

"I must confess the rest of it," he said. "I was lost, and yet, still I fought the idea of doing anything about it. I stupidly supposed it might be some sort of hopeless infatuation, something time might cure. Nevertheless, every day I thought of you endlessly. I wondered how you fared, and kept finding changes and additions that must be made in the folly for your comfort. I could not bear the thought of the fires dying, and checked them often. Twice, in fact, you nearly caught me at it. Once you appeared moments after I left. I was still on the far side of the clearing and would have been spotted had you looked in my direction. Another day, I was inside when I heard you on the step, and I dashed up the stairs and out onto the balcony, waiting there until you departed."

"But it has been so cold! I cannot bear the thought of you shivering out of doors while I dawdled!"

He turned back towards her then, smiling, but there was something desolate in it. "You are very kind, but my coat is quite warm, and you only stayed an hour or so. You were safely enjoying a respite I had helped create for you, I was as close to you as circumstances allowed, and I quite treasured it as time well spent."

"I had supposed you sent a trusted servant to tend the fires," she said softly. "The only time I thought differently was Thursday morning, when I fell asleep here. For some reason, I was quite convinced it was you who had come that day."

"It *was* I on Thursday and all but two other occasions. I went to London twice—once to fetch the chair and footstool from my Mayfair home. I knew the furniture would fit you perfectly, and Netherfield had nothing so comfortable, although it did provide the chaise longue. The second time, I went to purchase the writing desk. Both of those days, I had my man see to the fires until my return. He is both loyal and discreet, you may be assured. I admit, I resented the time away and not being able to attend to your comfort myself."

Touched, she smiled up at him; he did not return it.

"You believed, I understood," he continued, "that you had at least three weeks, and perhaps as long as three months or more before any betrothal was announced. I considered I had that much time to decide how I would act. By Thursday morning, I had concluded that my feelings for you were no mere infatuation. I was resolved, even anxious, to discover the details of your engagement, having no doubt that I could convince your potential bridegroom to withdraw. I asked you once to name him, and at that time, you would not."

The look of agony was back upon his face. "In the nine days we were apart, you lost weight. There were dark circles under your eyes from sleeplessness. Even though I tried to be quiet, I could not help making some slight noise, but you did not stir. I worried you were not merely asleep, but that your health had steeply declined. While I had been dithering about unimportant, stupid, selfish considerations the effects of marriage to you might have upon my consequence, you were *suffering*—suffering alone. I hated myself in that moment."

Elizabeth's eyes filled with tears. "I was never alone. I knew, whether you or your servant executed the actions, I was surrounded by your care, your attention, and your kindness when I was here. I felt you in every morsel of food left to tempt my appetite. This place was my respite, my source of reprieve and relief, but it was all you. *You* were my comfort. *You* were my peace."

He knelt at her feet. "Had that been all, I might be able to forgive myself. But then I read your letter." His throat worked. "Dash it, Elizabeth, it was Mr Goulding! I could not believe it."

She sought to explain. "He and my father are distant cousins on his mother's side. They have known each other all their lives and are good friends."

He met her gaze. "I am distantly related also. On my father's side."

Her brow furrowed as she tried to make the connexions fit. "But you cannot be the heir presumptive. It is an elderly man, from what my father told me." Other words from that seemingly long-ago conversation with her father came back to her. "Oh, but...*you* are the callous heir? That is impossible!"

"I called upon Mr Goulding when I learnt from my solicitors that I was next in line to inherit, after a cousin who is, apparently, quite ill. I ought never to have made the visit, not until I had myself under better regulation. It was, in that moment, unwelcome news. I had just received a letter from Georgiana, showing she was not in spirits. I was concerned that Bingley was becoming too involved with your sister, and I was already struggling with my feelings for you. I had decided that Bingley, his family, and I should return to London the day after the ball. And now here was this enormous obligation, one that would probably mean I was required to spend a good deal of time in Hertfordshire if I leased it or until I sold it. If I was here, Bingley would never resist the temptation to return to Miss Bennet. I behaved as though Mr Goulding was at death's door, and I should have to begin managing Haye-Park on the morrow!" He shook his head. "At any rate, Mr Goulding began going on at length about what a boon his estate would be to me, how fortunate I was, and I-I..." he trailed off, his head bowed.

Elizabeth touched his chin and raised it, letting him see her soft smile. "Did you tell him it was a tolerable estate, but not handsome enough to tempt you?"

"It was near enough." He turned his head and kissed her hand, closing his eyes, as though it hurt to look at her. "Elizabeth," he breathed. "I am so sorry. I had already behaved like a beast towards you, earning the contempt of the entire community. Wickham was maligning my name to anyone who would listen, and I refused to defend myself. I visited Mr Goulding the morning of the Netherfield ball. When I departed Haye-Park, I decided I deserved a reward for having performed my duty—it would be asking you to dance that evening." He sighed heavily. "But because of how I had acted, Mr Goulding went directly to your father, and they formed their plans.

Mr Goulding was desperate to save Haye-Park from a terrible overlord. What else was he to think? Had I been a better man, you would never have been made to suffer. How dare I ask you to forgive me?"

"Forgive you for what, sir? Do you mean for taking the time to consider your duty, your family obligations, before encouraging false hopes? For ensuring my peace, comfort, and safety, regardless of whether I ever became anything more to you than an acquaintance? I certainly expect no apology for you having endured whatever degradations you must have undertaken in order to reassure Mr Goulding. I see nothing to forgive in your behaviour."

She stood, forcing him to do likewise. Daringly, she placed her hand upon his shoulder.

"Oh, my dearest," he said, pulling her firmly into his embrace. "I am more wildly in love with you each day. My former hesitation makes no sense at all to me. You possessed my every thought, but I felt so helpless to provide anything useful for your succour. What did I know about pleasing a woman worthy of being pleased?"

"You know a little, Mr Darcy. Every day I found a treasure, and with it, another reason to love you."

She smiled, and he kissed into that smile—their mouths discovering, tasting, sharing, and learning. Elizabeth felt wholly new and radiantly happy.

It was only after she understood—by certain words and expressions of passionate affection—that he felt the same that she asked, "How did you make my father and Mr Goulding listen to you?"

He brushed a few stray locks away from her flushed cheek and raised a brow.

"After I read your letter, I composed one of my own, and sent it express to my uncle, who is the earl of Matlock. Fortunately, he is in town. I told him I was involved in some rather intense marital negotiations, and that I required a character."

Elizabeth's jaw dropped. "A character? As though you were applying for a household position? Oh my goodness!"

It was his turn to shrug. "I supposed that a reference from an earl, especially one with my uncle's excellent reputation, might mean a bit more to Mr Goulding than anything I could say in my defence. Unfortunately, I did not receive the earl's response until it was almost too late. I nearly had to go to Haye-Park without it. I only had perhaps fifteen or twenty minutes to present my apologies to Mr Goulding and to assure him a hasty marriage was completely unnecessary. He agreed only to discuss the matter with your father after dinner."

"Were you involved in that discussion?"

"Just to the extent that I repeated my apologies, reiterated the earl's estimation of my trustworthiness, and stated my opinion that my own unpardonable behaviour had led to their arrangement."

"But what about my father's debt? Papa told me Mr Goulding had called in his markers, and he either had to repay him or compel Jane or I to marry him."

"You had mentioned that there was another circumstance prohibiting your father's refusal, and I deduced a debt of some sort must be the case. I did not mention it to them, because I should not have known of any of this. I only told them that you had confessed the engagement to me the night of the ball, and it lately had occurred to me that the haste involved was related to my visit to Haye-Park that same day. I added that if there was any other sort of obligation between them, I would advance the amount necessary to cover it. Possibly, it was this additional pledge that rendered your father, at least, somewhat sceptical of my explanations of my involvement," Mr Darcy added wryly. "Neither of them was comfortable with speaking of the marriage as a requirement. If I had to guess, I would say 'the debt' was not one to be repaid in currency, but rather a debt of honour between friends."

"A debt of honour? I suppose that makes more sense than some enormous monetary debt. I admit, it is difficult not to resent that he used *me* to repay it."

"A father is accustomed to filial obedience. Like many men, I suppose he took it as his right that you fulfil any promises he made on your behalf."

She sighed. "So, you had to deal with my father as well? I am sorry for that." She imagined Mr Bennet had not kept secret his ill opinion of Mr Darcy.

"It was not so terrible. *Someone* had already begun the work of repairing his impression of me. I have noted a rather sudden about-face, so to speak, in the neighbourhood's sentiments towards Wickham and myself. Since I had told Bingley very little about my connexion to him, might I assume you had something to do with it?"

She shrugged. "I did not reveal much of what you told me, but it was enough to raise grave doubts as to his character. A flea in the ear of the right people ensured Mr Wickham would not be viewed as your benign victim, especially after the neighbourhood began making their own discoveries of him."

He kissed her again. "Yet another error on my part. After our discussion of his perfidies, I, too, informed a few others. I came to the unhappy conclusion that you had been correct. I was practically taught to protect him, and I had not considered how my silence was a continuation of it. I explained to both Mr Goulding and your father the true history of the living, and produced Wickham's release of all claims to it in exchange for payment. Once Mr Goulding was assured of my intent to protect the inhabitants of Haye-Park and ensure the estate's continued health, he seemed content enough. I am certain they have some suspicions that I am not a disinterested party where you are concerned, however."

"As you are not, I hope?"

"May I hope?" He held her face between his hands. Despite their size and strength, his touch was delicate and gentle. "May I go to your father?"

"Only if you wish to make me the happiest woman in the world—as the wife of Fitzwilliam Darcy must surely be."

"On my honour, it will be my life's mission to make it so," he replied, and then their mouths searched for anything and everything, except for words.

Elizabeth floated through the remainder of the day. She wondered whether Darcy—knowing she was in no danger of marrying anyone else— might wish for more time to consider his suit. But he was adamantly opposed to waiting, declaring his intention of speaking to her father at once. Thus, he accompanied her back to the stile, lifting her as he seemed to enjoy, but instead of immediately setting her down on the other side, he kissed her passionately.

"I have wanted to do that for so long," he murmured roughly. "I shall never tire of it. I will see you later this morning."

When he released her, Elizabeth was not certain the ground was steady beneath her feet.

By day's end, she was engaged, and the planning for the wedding clothes began. Mrs Bennet was beside herself with joy, Lydia and Kitty were pressing for a ball as well as a wedding breakfast, and only Mary calmly commenting, "Your betrothed does not seem elderly to me," with a knowing look that told Elizabeth she had figured out much more than had been revealed to her.

Her father seemed resigned. After Darcy departed, he called her into his book-room. "Why did you not tell me Mr Darcy was in love with you?"

"I did not know it," she replied. "I suppose it was only hearing of my possible betrothal to another that helped him determine his feelings for me were serious."

He considered her for some moments, and she wondered whether he would ask all the questions he must surely have.

"Will you forgive me for forcing the betrothal to Goulding upon you? I shall always feel that it was not the cruelty you took it to be, but in retrospect, I can see how, in the haste with which I acted, it must have seemed so."

It was not enough, a mere nod to her feelings of loss and loneliness. "For what am I to forgive you?" she said sharply, asking the question for the second time that day. "For ordering me to marry without warning, without discussion, without choice, to a man I consider an uncle? For your disingenuous account of our family's ruin if I did not?" Her anger faded, her voice softening as sadness replaced it. "Or for your sudden refusal to be the papa I have always known, the man who has always protected me, reasoned with me, valued, trusted, and stood by me. I thought you always would." A single tear slipped down her cheek, but she impatiently wiped it away.

Mr Bennet opened his mouth as if to protest, but then he closed it again. For some moments, the only sound was the mantel clock's measured beat in the silence. Elizabeth would not fill it; she had said her piece.

He sighed, his shoulders slumping. "I deserve your anger, I think," he said quietly. "I do not know how I shall earn your understanding or forgiveness. I cannot seem to manage it for myself at the moment."

On Sunday, the village church was turned upon its ear when the banns were called for *both* Mr Bingley and Jane and Mr Darcy and Elizabeth, the vicar having fortunately agreed to change the name of one of the grooms upon very short notice. The two gentlemen took full advantage of their new status as family members to spend the Sabbath at Longbourn, and Elizabeth rejoiced in planning a future which had suddenly grown bright.

Monday morning, nearly the entire family—including Mr Bingley and Darcy—awaited the arrival of Mr Collins in the drawing room. Mr Bennet absented himself, refusing to either encourage or discourage Mary's choice, which was rather hypocritical, Elizabeth felt. Kitty and Lydia were giggling with each other, ignoring everyone else, and Mary was, for once, at the centre of her mother's attention.

"Do not quote scripture to him, Mary—unless it is one of the 'wife, submit to your husband' verses. Gentlemen love those."

"Mama, you take those verses out of context if you

do not explain the greater obligations of the man towards—"

"I am trying to explain how to hold a man's interest, not hold a Bible study—"

"I apologise for my family," Elizabeth whispered to Darcy. "Mary and Mama often speak at cross purposes. Usually they just ignore each other."

"You look beautiful this morning," he whispered back, and Elizabeth realised he could not care less about the bickering. She gave him a brilliant smile.

Mr Collins was expected to arrive on the morning post; Mr Bingley had kindly sent his carriage into Meryton to await the honoured guest. To their collective surprise, instead of Mr Bingley's vehicle, an unfamiliar chaise-and-four pulled up the drive, drawing the attention of everyone to the windows.

Mr Bingley looked puzzled. "Who can that be? It is too early for visitors."

The ladies began conjecturing, but it was Darcy who answered, his words clipped. "It is my aunt, Lady Catherine de Bourgh. It appears that Mr Collins has not come alone, though I do not understand why she felt it necessary to accompany him."

"My dear Miss Bennet," Mr Bingley announced, leaping to his feet, "Were you not going to show me the hermitage this morning?"

"Oh, I did not—" Jane said, but he clasped her hand and practically dragged her from the room.

"Ah," Mary said. "Mr Collins's esteemed patroness. I suppose I shall gain first-hand answers to my questions regarding her disposition. This ought to be interesting."

"You have no idea," Darcy muttered.

Elizabeth looked at him; he was standing behind her chair, his attention drawn to the windows, looking thunderous.

"Darcy?" she murmured, a sudden frisson of nerves making her shiver.

He placed a hand upon her shoulder, and she covered it with her own. Although his expression remained grim, his eyes crinkled as he looked down upon her—his version of a comforting smile.

A few moments later, Mr Collins entered the drawing room accompanied by a large, tall woman who might once have been handsome.

She spotted Darcy immediately. She gaped at him—and at his hand, which he had not removed from Elizabeth's shoulder—with narrowed eyes.

"Nephew," she said, her voice rigid. She peered down her nose at Elizabeth. "I suppose you are Miss Elizabeth Bennet."

"Shall I make you known to her and her family, your ladyship?" asked Darcy.

Lady Catherine blinked several times, as though she could not believe the words he had just spoken. She addressed her next words to Mrs Bennet. "You are her mother?"

"Yes, madam. Elizabeth is my eldest but one, and these are—"

Lady Catherine interrupted Mrs Bennet's attempt

to make introductions. "You have a very small park here. Darcy, I should be glad to take a turn in it with *Miss Elizabeth Bennet*, if she will favour me with her company." She pronounced Elizabeth's name as though the syllables were poison on her tongue.

Elizabeth was astonished by Lady Catherine's manner. She took some comfort in Darcy's immediate reply.

"Miss Elizabeth requires no man's permission to walk out on her own lawn with anyone. Should you believe, however, that *you* have *my* permission to speak to her with anything less than the greatest civility, you will find yourself quite mistaken."

Lady Catherine's nostrils flared. "I received a most alarming report from my brother, *his lordship*," she said, adding the honorific with particular emphasis. "I insist upon having it contradicted."

Mr Collins, Elizabeth noted, hovered near the doorway, watching his patroness with wide eyes. It was as though he was waiting for a signal that he might more fully enter the drawing room. Lady Catherine gave none.

"If it is the report of my intention to marry Miss Elizabeth, I can give you no contradiction. I have proposed, and she has accepted me."

"Darcy! How can you so completely forget your obligations to your cousin Anne, not to mention those to me, for your mother's sake!"

Elizabeth regarded Darcy, her brows raised. He appeared pained.

"If you had hopes in that quarter, you know I have never encouraged them."

Lady Catherine turned her piercing stare upon Elizabeth. "This is not to be borne. I hope she does not expect to be noticed by your family or friends. Why would we recognise her when she wilfully acts against the inclinations of all? Your alliance will be a disgrace. Her name will never be mentioned by any of us."

Even Kitty and Lydia were finally paying attention enough to look dumbfounded.

"Therein ends my life's aspirations," Elizabeth muttered under her breath.

"What did she say? Darcy, tell her to repeat herself. I must know."

He scowled and took a step towards his aunt. "The only thing you must know is that *I* shall not notice *you*, or anyone else who insults my bride. I have informed the earl, my solicitors, and the vicar. It is done, as is your visit here. I caution you not to return until you recall the manners of a lady. Your behaviour disrespects my mother and your entire family."

Lady Catherine's brows flew up nearly to her hairline, fury lighting her countenance. For a moment, Elizabeth thought she might hit someone. Darcy might have believed something similar, for he stepped forward, ensuring Elizabeth was behind him.

After a heavy pause, Lady Catherine whirled around and flounced out of the room.

Mr Collins at last advanced into the room. "Um.

Miss Mary, I wonder, whether you might care to walk out with me. The day promises fine."

Mary solemnly nodded, excusing herself to fetch her coat.

Through the window, Elizabeth saw the shiny black chaise-and-four departing.

The room grew quiet, apparently not even Kitty and Lydia knowing what to say. After they heard the front door shut behind Mr Collins and Mary, Darcy addressed Mrs Bennet. "I apologise for my aunt's rudeness, madam."

Mrs Bennet, however, barely acknowledged the words in her haste to crowd with Lydia and Kitty at the window, eagerly watching Mr Collins and Mary walking upon the lawn.

"Three weddings!" Mrs Bennet sighed.

"Oh, Mama, how do you think she can listen to him without laughing?" Lydia wondered.

Kitty giggled.

Elizabeth—torn between shock at Lady Catherine's behaviour and her family's overlooking of it, as well as gratitude that they somehow had—held her hand out to Darcy. Instead of taking it, he drew her into his arms, standing behind her, his big body warming her along her back. She felt a kiss upon her neck which travelled through her entire being. No one was paying them the slightest bit of attention, but still she could hardly believe he dared it.

"I am desperately in love with you," he whispered in her ear, sending chills up and down her spine. In the next moment his arms fell away, and when she glanced over her shoulder at him, he was once again standing impassively, watching her mother and sisters with what she once would have supposed was disdain. Knowing him as she had come to, she understood his expression meant he was not seeing them at all.

"Oh, look, they are returning," Kitty cried. "So quickly!"

"He does not take her arm," Lydia noted. "He is very red in the face."

Mrs Bennet waved this off. "You cannot possibly see such particulars from here. His hat is casting a shadow, that is all."

"They are walking at least three feet apart."

"You exaggerate, Kitty. I am certain the gap is half that," Mrs Bennet insisted. She and her two youngest daughters began bickering about the exact distance between the couple.

Darcy drew Elizabeth against him again, his hands at her shoulders. "How soon can we marry?" he murmured.

"Are you not eager to learn the state of Mary's romance?"

"What I am eager for is so wildly inappropriate in our current setting, I can hardly believe I have the temerity to remain in this room."

She blushed, but the truth was, she wished for the same things. "You know Jane and Mr Bingley set their date for mid-March, to give Mama the time to make it as splendid a celebration as this neighbourhood has ever seen. I suppose we need not have a double wedding, if you do not wish it."

"You would be willing that I should get a licence and be married within a week?" he asked hopefully.

Laughing softly, she turned to face him. "I was hoping that my wedding clothes would be finished before I became your wife."

"I will hire a dozen seamstresses to make it so."

She reached up to touch his cheek, delighting in the feel of it as his hands briefly tightened on her shoulders. "When Mr Bingley and Jane announced their betrothal, it was Mama who decided when it would be. They are both too kind to overrule her. Perhaps you would be willing to persuade your friend that he does not wish to remain unwed for quite so many months as that? You could fetch your sister here for Christmas, and we could be married in two weeks' time and bring in the New Year together as man and wife."

He covered her hand with his. "That would be agreeable beyond anything. I will persuade Bingley, whatever it takes. Will you be able to convince your sister?"

"Oh, please. I suspect she might love Mr Bingley almost as much as I do you," she replied smilingly. "She cannot be anything except happy to wed him sooner."

"Where could they be going?" Mrs Bennet cried so loudly that Darcy and Elizabeth turned their attention back to the windows.

Mary and Mr Collins were disappearing down the drive in the direction of the village.

"Perhaps they wish to see Aunt Philips?" Kitty suggested. "Or they could be going to purchase her wedding clothes."

"That makes little sense," Lydia protested. "Why would she announce her betrothal to our aunt before us? Bringing him shopping with her would be even stupider."

"My poor nerves!" Mrs Bennet moaned. "No one ever considers them!"

At that moment, Jane and Mr Bingley re-entered the room; Lydia quickly apprised them of the mystery.

"Oh, my," Jane said. "I cannot imagine what Mary is doing."

"I believe I know," Elizabeth interjected. "I think she is bringing Mr Collins to Lucas Lodge."

All six of her companions looked at her with varying levels of curiosity.

"She intends to introduce him—or re-introduce him —to Charlotte," Elizabeth explained.

"Why would she do such a thing?" Mrs Bennet demanded. It took just a moment for her to understand what Elizabeth was implying. Her expression darkened, and she cried, "No! She cannot! I must stop her!" Mrs Bennet stepped towards the door as though she meant to chase the couple down.

Speaking loudly enough for everyone to hear, Darcy said, "Bingley, would you and Miss Bennet be willing to advance the wedding date, to, let us say, two weeks from today?"

The question had the immediate effect of diverting Mrs Bennet's attention away from Mary and Mr Collins.

The resulting commotion filled the room with exclamations and excitement. Mrs Bennet forgot her intention of wresting Mr Collins to the ground and forcing a different answer from her daughter once both gentlemen assured their future mother-in-law she need have no worries for her future, regardless of Mary's decision. By the time the discussion was settled, Elizabeth was not quite sure her mother remembered a proposal and its refusal had taken place, and the new wedding date was secured.

"I almost made a terrible mistake," Mary admitted, speaking to Elizabeth later in the privacy of her chamber. "I accepted Mr Collins's word regarding the intelligence and rationality of Lady Catherine, and was inclined to accept him. How stupid must she be to believe that she could possibly alter Mr Darcy's opinion of you in such a senseless manner, by a means so ham-handed and coarse as to surely put his back up!"

"Since Lady Catherine apparently abandoned Mr Collins to us, I thought perhaps he was not of the same mind as his patroness."

"Oh, he always planned to take the post home, for he meant to stay a few nights, and her ladyship did not. Of course, had Mr Collins been as appalled with her behaviour as I was, I would not have blamed him for her actions. Instead, he began by advising me that I must warn my sister against following through with a marriage to which she had already committed! Apparently, Lady Catherine spent the entire journey to Longbourn lecturing him on how he was to use his influence with me to force you to change your mind, lest he change his."

"That was certainly...bold."

"I told him that if the price of his happiness was the ruin of another's, *he* might be glad to pay it, but *I* would not. I also suggested several verses of scripture he might wish to study regarding the fate of those who put their own selfish desires ahead of their fellow man, and none of which were about *submission*. Then I asked him whether he remembered meeting Charlotte Lucas, who might have more patience with his self-interest than I do."

It was all Elizabeth could do to suppress a giggle. "Well said, Mary! Thank you for your defence of my engagement and my feelings. I do hope Mr Collins was not so upset as to be less than dignified in his response."

Mary appeared thoughtful. "I believe he was a bit embarrassed, because he knew I was correct. At the same time, I suppose he realised that I would not make him a very comfortable wife."

"Was he offended at the mention of Charlotte?"

"No, not at all. He was certain they had been introduced but could not recall her face, thus I offered to bring him to Lucas Lodge to present him again. Charlotte, of course, was very agreeable to him, and I escaped as soon as I could. He might have watched me go with a bit of regret, but he will accustom himself to a change of spouses, I have no doubt."

"What of you? Are you disappointed not to be marrying yet?"

Mary gave it serious thought—as she did everything. "I believe I am disappointed that he was not the man I hoped he could be. But it is best to know it now, before one is committed to a life of misery, is it not?"

Elizabeth pledged herself, then and there, to do her utmost to look after Mary's future happiness. As she lay in bed that night, she reflected how much better it was to be astonished by a lover's goodness than to be disillusioned by his flaws.

Epilogue

I t was the final day of the year. The wedding breakfast was attended, Elizabeth observed, by most of the neighbourhood, and Netherfield's dining parlour was full to overflowing. If her mother had been unable to do everything she wanted to, she had certainly done more than enough. Mr Goulding sent a lovely gift, a set of Sèvres porcelain dishes elegant enough to serve royalty. It was accompanied by a note wishing Elizabeth and Darcy every joy. The idea had occurred to her that within a year or two, Mary—pragmatic and the opposite of Elizabeth in nearly every way—might very well be longing to have her own home and could be happy as Mrs Goulding. Mr Goulding was, as her father had insisted, not so elderly as she had once asserted, and Mary was an old soul. Well, she would see what she and Darcy could do, and no matter what, Mary's choices would always remain her own.

Mr Collins and his soon-to-be-bride, Charlotte, were here with the rest of the Lucases. He had returned to Meryton yesterday, presumably as eager to escape the wrath of his patroness as to attend the nuptials. If he glanced at Mary occasionally with longing in his eyes, neither Charlotte nor Mary seemed to notice.

Lydia and Kitty were unusually subdued. After the discovery several days before of a letter from Mr Wickham to Lydia—with Kitty complicit in the correspondence—their father, acting on the advice of Darcy and with his assistance, had immediately hired them a sort of governess-companion. Miss Shaw was a sensible individual who they were rapidly learning was not to be crossed, and yet who was spirited and wise enough to help them occupy their minds with more than flirtations. The youngest Bennets had been promised visits to London and a much broader social sphere, but only with great improvement to their manners and general behaviour.

Toasts to the happy couples were offered by many— amusing ones, such as his gregarious cousin the colonel proposed, and touching ones as well: Mr Bennet's humble words of love and relief took Elizabeth another few steps towards forgiveness. Even Georgiana had shyly offered a pledge of her great happiness for her brother and new sister, if a quiet one, heard only by them. If Mrs Hurst and Miss Bingley did not appear overly enthusiastic, they were at least gracious and mannerly and had offered Mrs Bennet every assistance in planning the event.

Mrs Bennet looked about her with shining eyes; in Elizabeth's opinion, having two daughters married, and to such rich men, had a wonderful effect upon her mother's health. She appeared years younger than she had only a few weeks previous, almost sparkling—and Elizabeth saw her father noticing the alteration, too, with less of sarcasm and more of interest than was his wont.

It was Darcy, however, who brought tears to Elizabeth's eyes. It was after all those who had raised a glass had finished speaking and Mr Bingley made a little speech thanking everyone for coming to share in their happiness. Elizabeth had even begun to wonder whether she could slip upstairs to change into her new—and very smart—carriage dress. She was excited to be on her way to London, where she and Darcy would begin married life together. They would go to Pemberley as soon as the weather was more certain.

Darcy stood, and such was his natural eminence and gravity, that the room immediately quieted.

"It is a truth, universally acknowledged, that I did not begin on the best footing in this neighbourhood," he said, eliciting a few chuckles. "I would like to publicly retract a statement I thoughtlessly made once upon a time and offer a different one. My wife, Mrs Elizabeth Darcy, is the most beautiful creature in the world, in case anyone was in doubt of my feelings on the matter." There was laughter, applause, and even a whistle or two, probably from one of the youngest Lucas boys, judging by the way Lady Lucas appeared to be scolding them.

Darcy looked at Elizabeth, his deep chocolate gaze unwavering; for a moment there was no one else in the room, before he again addressed them all.

"When I was young, I was very badly used. Due to those experiences, I was on guard against most everyone.

There were very few able to see past that—but thank you, Bingley, for trying."

There was more laughter, but it was softer, less... humorous, somehow.

"A man who trusts no one can love no one. Oh, he might peer over the top of the wall which surrounds him to occasionally admire another—but no, there is not room within such a fortress to be vulnerable, to be open, to allow others to know him. The only person whose feelings truly matter is one's own self. Such I was, from seven to seven and twenty, determined to never prove myself a fool again, and such I might still have been—remaining aloof and closed off for the rest of my life, had not my eyes been opened to true beauty, courage, wit, and kindness by the new Mrs Darcy."

Elizabeth reached up to take his hand. He squeezed it, but he was not finished, and drew her up to his side, looking into her eyes.

"It is very likely that I shall say many stupid things in the course of what I pray is a very long life together." There were a few more chuckles.

She smiled up at him. "Surely not."

He did not return her smile. "Knowing this, I beg leave to pledge, before all these witnesses, a vow in addition to the ones I made before God this morning. I will replace my guard against all and sundry with trust in everyone, at least until they prove unworthy of it."

Her mouth opened, just a little, in surprise. "I am not certain, husband, that such a...a conviction is wise."

In his way—really, just with his eyes—he smiled

back. "Most would call it remarkably foolish. My trust will, doubtlessly, at times be abused. But not by every person, and besides, who am I *not* to be ill-used? It would be better, I think, to remain open to confidence in my fellow man and retain the respect and expectations of my dearest, loveliest wife, than to choose a safer caution and defence against knowing anybody."

A voice in the crowd—she was fairly certain it was her uncle Gardiner—cried out, "Hear, hear!"

For a moment, her throat closed. No one present, except herself and possibly Georgiana, understood how he had been hurt and what the vow he had just made would cost him. What could she offer him in return for such a promise? She looked out at the crowd of friends, family, and neighbours. Was it her imagination that everyone appeared a bit warmer, a bit kinder than usual? Or was it only her own joy, colouring them all?

"I would like everyone here to know that Mr Darcy has already apologised, a number of times, for any poorly chosen words he might have spoken before learning that we in Meryton are the most honourable lot in England."

Soft laughter greeted her words, as she thanked the company for coming to celebrate with them. "You can all see what perfections I shall have to endure. There are many who might remind him that he did not marry so high as he could have. However, in a man so good, it does not matter. No one *could* be truly worthy of him, but I have him, and I shall keep him."

He shook his head in both amusement and discomfiture at the applause of the company. Shortly thereafter, the guests began drifting out onto Netherfield's terrace, separating into smaller groups.

Elizabeth could not fail to notice that several of her neighbours made their way to Darcy afterwards. She tensed a little, wondering whether his rash and reckless pledge had already borne ill fruits. Yet, it seemed only that they wanted to make themselves further known to him, reaching out with a hand of friendship. It took a much longer time than she had expected to extricate them both from well-wishers, and it was the afternoon before they found themselves in a carriage making its way towards London. As Colonel Fitzwilliam was returning Georgiana to his parents at Matlock, they were alone together for the first time since their engagement.

She suddenly felt a little shy. It seemed rather impossible that the beautiful man sitting beside her, holding her hand in silence, could actually be her husband.

"I have a wedding gift for you," he said after several minutes, "although it is not ready yet. As soon as the weather clears, a new folly shall be constructed at Pemberley. I think you can guess its design in every particular."

She looked up at him in amazement. "You are too generous, sir. I dare not present you with my simple offering now."

He looked at her with interest. "Please do."

From the seat beside her, she withdrew a bound notebook; he smiled.

"Is this one from your writing desk?" he asked.

"Yes. When you had it delivered to me at Long-bourn, I knew at once what I wished to do with it."

She handed him the notebook, slightly embarrassed, watching as he opened it to the inscription.

"'With Appreciation to my Beloved'," he read aloud, gazing up at her. "You have written your book after all."

"It is the story of how I came to know your good heart."

He raised a brow. "It is a most unusual tale. I would think you might better wish to forget some of those memories, however."

"Not at all. I told you, at my lowest point, when I believed I might never again be able to recognise 'anything lovely or praiseworthy or of good report', that it might help to have a book containing long lists of possibilities."

"So I recall."

"We cannot promise each other that we shall never again face times of misery or despair. If we do, I want us to remember that *we* experienced a miracle during just such a time. I want to keep this memory within reach, always. I think it would be much more effective in renewing hope and gratitude than a book of random lists."

He did not respond, only began reading. After several minutes, he carefully closed the notebook.

When he said nothing, Elizabeth began to feel uncomfortable. When the idea had occurred to her, it had seemed a way of expressing her love, but perhaps it was merely childish.

"It is odd, is it not?" she asked him, once she gathered her composure. "We are now free to live the rest of our lives together, and yet we do not really know each other. The important aspects of character we understand, I believe, but there are many details between the vows we made this morning and every other day that follows. Where do I even begin?"

In a motion as surprising to her as the first time he had lifted her over the stile, he set the notebook aside and swept her up and onto his lap. With an astonishing competency, he removed her hat and gloves and kissed her just as he had in the folly—slow and impassioned, worshipfully, and sweetly. There was no restraint needed, but he took his time exploring her mouth, her throat, behind her ears and across her collarbones with a teasing sensuality and tender control.

"Let us start with this, and I believe the rest will come to me as we go along," he said, his deep voice solemn, but the smile was back in his eyes, crinkling at their corners, as she wrapped her arms around him.

"I am already learning, I suppose, how my husband thinks," she said, not hiding her return smile. "What is most important to him, his needs, and his desires."

His gaze grew serious, and he set one hand upon the notebook. "I shall treasure this, my love, above every volume in Pemberley's library. I hope you will never again be so utterly alone as you were during the period it covers—not simply because we are married, but that I shall grow more attuned to *you*, to your needs and your desires, with every passing day. If I ignore or neglect any of them, I hope you will tell me. If you wonder what is most important to me? It is you, always you. Forever you."

"'And the two shall become one'," she quoted softly. "An ever deeper understanding with a lifetime's worth of loyalty and effort. I suppose that is what it truly means to never be alone."

His mouth descended to hers and then there were no more words, as they began life's journey together.

The End

GET A FREE EBOOK!

Receive a free ebook when you sign up for the publisher's newsletter! *For the Enjoyment of Reading* contains short stories by Jan Ashton, Julie Cooper, Amy D'Orazio, Linda Gonschior, Lucy Marin, and Mary Smythe. Its yours, free, for signing up for the Quills & Quartos Newsletter.

Get it at www. QuillsandQuartos.com

ACKNOWLEDGMENTS

Deepest thanks to Lucy Marin, Amy D'Orazio, and Jan Ashton for editing prowess. This little book had some wonderful input from each.

ABOUT THE AUTHOR

Julie Cooper, a California native, lives with her Mr Darcy (without the arrogance or the Pemberley) of nearly forty years, two dogs (one intelligent, one goofball), and Kevin the Cat (smarter than all of them.) They have four children and four grandchildren, all of whom are brilliant and adorable, and she has the pictures to prove it. She works as an executive at a gift basket company and her tombstone will read, 'Have your Christmas gifts delivered at least four days before the 25th.' Her hobbies include reading, giving other people good advice, and wondering why no one follows it.

To be first to learn of Julie's new releases follow her on Amazon and BookBub.

ALSO BY JULIE COOPER

NOVELS

A Stronger Impulse

Nameless

Tempt Me

The Perfect Gentleman

NOVELLAS

A Yuletide Dream

Lost and Found

Seek Me: Georgiana's Story

A companion novella to Tempt Me

MULTI-AUTHOR PROJECTS

'Tis the Season

A Match Made at Matlock